Charles Gounod, Annette E Crocker

Memoirs of an Artist

An Autobiography

Charles Gounod, Annette E Crocker

Memoirs of an Artist
An Autobiography

ISBN/EAN: 9783337027841

Printed in Europe, USA, Canada, Australia, Japan

Cover: Foto ©Raphael Reischuk / pixelio.de

More available books at **www.hansebooks.com**

CHARLES FRANÇOIS GOUNOD.

MEMOIRS OF AN ARTIST

An Autobiography

BY

CHARLES FRANÇOIS GOUNOD

RENDERED INTO ENGLISH
BY
ANNETTE E. CROCKER

CHICAGO AND NEW YORK:
RAND, McNALLY & COMPANY.
MDCCCXCV.

TRANSLATOR'S PREFACE.

Gounod, in these memoirs, terms words "docile and faithful servants of thought," and states their duty to be to "lead one to the summit without rude shock—mysterious guides, who conceal both themselves and their methods."

Words served him thus. He was their master, as he was master of all things he took in hand to perform, his dominating genius attuning thought to phrase as sweetly as it wove melody and harmony into musical expression.

I approached with trepidation the task of clothing in new livery his deft servitors, fearing that, perchance, ill-fashioned apparel might render their presence obvious, their guidance clumsy; nevertheless, I undertook the work, actuated by a resolute purpose to maintain faithfully the tone of the original.

That I have fallen somewhat short in my aim, I am only too conscious, but that the substance and color of the master's thought are at least faintly reflected, I fain would hope.

The abrupt termination of his memoirs, which break off at a time before the tardy public fully recognized his genius, is a matter of deep regret, for his illuminating comments on contemporary compositions and men doubtless would have been of inestimable value and interest.

It is believed that he brought his memoirs down much nearer to the present time, but afterward destroyed the latter part. Many theories are advanced to account for this regrettable destruction, the most plausible of which is based on the knowledge that shortly after the production of *Faust* there occurred phases in his life which probably he later desired to forget; so it may be reasonably assumed that, dreading to embitter with distressing memories the mellow joys of subsequent years of prosperous recognition, he blotted out that part of his autobiography which would have recalled painful episodes.

Whatever may have been the cause, the loss, though great, is, fortunately, not altogether irreparable; for Gounod was a voluminous correspondent, and his letters, which it is understood will soon be published, will in some measure compensate for the loss of his later memoirs.

ANNETTE E. CROCKER.

CHICAGO, December, 1895.

PREFACE.

The following pages tell of the events that have most affected my life as an artist, of the impressions that I have received, of the influence they have exercised upon my career, and the reflections they have suggested to me.

Without deceiving myself as to the degree of interest that may attach to my personality, I believe that the precise and simple relation of the life of an artist may afford to others useful instruction, which, lying concealed, perhaps, in some fact or word of no apparent importance, adapts itself to individuals according to the disposition of the mind or the needs of the moment. The most unimportant action, the most unpremeditated word, often exerts a beneficial influence; this has been my experience, and what has been useful or salutary to me may be so to others.

(5)

An author, in writing memoirs, has frequent, almost momentary, occasion to speak of himself. In doing this I have tried to be impartial in the expression of my opinions; I have endeavored to be exact and truthful in the narration of events, especially when repeating the words of others concerning me. I have stated with sincerity what I think of my own works; but the owl deceives herself in her judgment of her little ones, and I am no better protected than she from the danger of delusion. Time, if it should occupy itself with me, will decide the measure of my worth; upon it I depend to put me where I belong, as it does with all things else, or to set me right if I be out of place.

This account of my life is a testimony of veneration and affection for the being who has given me the greatest love in the world — mother-love. The mother is, here below, the most perfect image, the purest and warmest ray of Providence; her never-failing care and watchfulness are the direct emanation of the eternal care and watchfulness of God.

If I have succeeded in being, saying, or doing anything good, however small, in my life, it is to my mother that I owe it; and it is to her that I wish to give the credit. It was she who nursed me, who brought me up, who formed me — not, alas, in her own image; that would have been too beautiful — and in whatever respect I may have lacked, the shortcoming was not hers, but mine.

She rests under a stone as pure and simple as was her life.

May this tribute of a well-beloved son leave upon her tomb a wreath more durable than our "immortelles of a day," and assure for her memory, after my death, a respect that I could wish to make eternal!

MEMOIRS OF AN ARTIST.

I.

CHILDHOOD.

My mother was born at Rouen, June 4, 1780, her maiden name being Victoire Lemachois. Her father was a magistrate of that city. Her mother, a Mademoiselle Heuzey, was endowed with remarkable intelligence and a wonderful gift for the arts. She was a poet and musician; she composed, sang, and played the harp; and I have often heard my mother say that she acted tragedy like Mademoiselle Duchesnois, and comedy like Mademoiselle Mars.

Such a rare combination of exceptional natural gifts made her sought for by the most distinguished persons in high society, such as the families

of d'Houdetot, de Mortemart, Saint-
Lambert, d'Herbouville, and others,
among whom she was literally a
spoiled child.

But, alas! the accomplishments
which are the charm and fascination
of life do not always insure happiness.
Domestic peace is with difficulty preserved in the case of a total disparity
of tastes, inclinations, and instincts,
and it is a dangerous dream to wish
to subject the realities of life to the
reign of the ideal. Thus, harmony
was not slow in deserting a household
where so many differences conspired
to banish it. My mother's childhood
suffered the unhappy consequence,
and her life became serious at the age
when she should have known no care.

But God had blessed her, however,
with a strong mind, good sense, and
courage equal to anything. Deprived
at an early age of a mother's care, she
was obliged to learn alone to read and
write, and acquired by herself, also,
the first ideas of drawing and music,

of the latter of which she was soon to make use as a source of livelihood.

The Revolution occasioned my grandfather the loss of his position in the court of Rouen. My mother then thought only of striving to be useful. She sought for piano pupils, which having found, she commenced, at the age of eleven years, that laborious profession to which, when later a widow, she was to have recourse as a means of raising her children.

Stimulated by a desire to always do better, and by a sense of duty that directed and dominated her whole life, she felt, as a teacher, the necessity of learning from the best authority the most correct method of instruction. She resolved, therefore, to have lessons from some celebrated master, by which means her reputation would be strengthened and her conscience reassured. In order to attain this object, she put aside, little by little—*sou* by *sou*, perhaps—a part of the poor little sum realized from her modest patronage, and, when she had saved the necessary amount, she took the coach, which was then three days in going from Rouen to Paris, and went straight to Adam, professor of piano at the Conservatory, also father of Adolphe Adam, author of *Le Chalet*, and of many other charming works. Adam received her kindly and listened to her with attention, recognizing in her the qualities that maintain and solidify the interest first felt in promising talent. Not being able, on account of her youth, to install herself in Paris for the purpose of taking lessons in a regular and consecutive manner, it was arranged that she should make the journey from Rouen to Paris once every three months to have a lesson.

One lesson every three months! That would hardly seem enough, it must be admitted, to be profitable. But there are beings who are a living demonstration of the miracle of the increase of bread in the wilderness,

and it will be seen by many other in-
stances in the course of this narrative,
that my mother was one of those
beings.

This woman, who was to win for
herself in after years so good and
genuine a reputation in teaching, was
not, *could not* be, a pupil to lose anything of the rare and precious instructions of her master. Therefore,
he was astonished at the progress
made from one lesson to another ; and
appreciating the courage of his young
pupil even more highly than her musical capacity, he obtained for her the
gratuitous possession of a piano, thus
enabling her to study assiduously
without the care and expense of hir-
ing one, which, little as the latter
might be, was still a great tax upon
her slender income.

Some time afterward, an event
occurred in my mother's life that
had a decisive effect upon her future.

The masters for piano music at
that time in vogue were Clementi,

Steibelt, Dussek, etc. I make no mention in this connection of Mozart, who, following Haydn, was already shining upon the musical world ; nor of the great Sebastian Bach, whose immortal collection of preludes and fugues, known as the "Well-Tempered Clavichord," had been for a century the unrivaled code for the study of the piano, and the breviary of musical composition. Beethoven, young yet, had not attained the celebrity that his giant genius was to conquer for him.

It was then that a celebrated German musician—Hullmandel, a violinist of great merit, and a friend and contemporary of Beethoven—came to France with the intention of obtaining pupils in accompaniment. Stopping at Rouen, he wished to hear some of the young 'people most advanced in musical art. A sort of competition was opened, in which my mother took part, and had the honor of being particularly remarked and congratulated by Hullmandel, who selected her at once as capable of receiving his instructions, and of being heard with him in houses where music was passionately and seriously cultivated.

At this point concludes the information obtained from my mother regarding her childhood and youth. I know no more of her life until the event of her marriage, which took place in 1806, she being then twenty-six and a half years old.

My father, François-Louis Gounod, born in 1758, was, at the time of his marriage, forty-seven years old. He was a distinguished painter, and my mother often told me that he was considered the best draughtsman of his time, by the great contemporary artists, Gérard, Girodet, Guérin, Joseph Vernet, Gros, and others. I recall a saying of Gérard's, repeated by my mother with justifiable pride. This artist, surrounded with glory and honors, baron of the empire, and possessor of a great fortune, had very fine equipages. Riding one day in his carriage, he met my father going on foot through the streets of Paris, upon which he immediately cried out:

"Gounod on foot, while I go in a carriage! Ah, that is a shame!"

My father was a pupil of Lépicié at the same time with Carle Vernet (son of Joseph and father of Horace). He twice competed for the *grand prix de Rome*. An act of his youth, in connection with one of these competitions, will show the scrupulous nature of his conscience, and his modesty as an artist and fellow-student. The subject chosen was "The Adulterous Woman." Among the competitors with whom he took part was the painter, Drouais, whose well-known remarkable picture of that name earned for him the great prize. Drouais had permitted my father to see his competing work.

The latter declared honestly to his comrade that there was no possible comparison between their pictures, and returning to his studio, he stripped up his own canvas, judging it unworthy to appear by the side of that of Drouais. This incident shows the high degree of his artistic integrity, which hesitated not an instant between the voice of justice and that of personal interest.

A man of learning, with fine perceptions and a highly cultivated mind, my father had, nevertheless, all his life, a sort of fear of undertaking any great work. Gifted as he was, it is, perhaps, to his frail health that we must look for an explanation of this reluctance. Allowance should also be made for his love of independence, the extreme need of which made him doubtful of engaging in a work of long duration. The following anecdote will furnish an example of this feeling:

Monsieur Denon, then conservator

2

of the Museum of the Louvre, and at the same time, I believe, superintendent of the Royal Museums of France, had a great personal liking for my father, and valued very highly his ability as a draughtsman and etcher. One day he proposed to the latter the execution of a number of etchings representing the collection comprising the cabinet of medals in the Louvre, and assuring him as a recompense for the finished work an annual income of 10,000 francs. For a household possessing nothing, that was, especially in those times, a fortune; and there were husband, wife, and two children to be maintained. But my father flatly refused this offer, limiting himself to the filling of orders for portraits and lithographs, of which several are works of the first rank, preserved to this day in families·for which they were executed.

Moreover, in the case of these very portraits, revealing a feeling so fine and a talent so marked, my mother's indomitable energy was often indispensable in bringing the task to a conclusion. How many of them would have rested by the way if she had not put her hand to the work? How many times was she, herself, obliged to clean and prepare the palette? And this was not all. As long as it was the question of the human in the portrait—the pose, the face, expression, eyes, look, the interior being, in fact—it was all pleasure, all enjoyment. But when it came to the details of the accessories—sleeves, ornaments, trimmings, insignia, etc. —oh, that was the time of weakness! there was no more interest; patience was necessary; and it was then that the poor wife took the brush and assumed the ungrateful part of the task, finishing by intelligence and courage the work commenced by talent and abandoned through dread of tedium.

My father, besides his work as a

painter, had consented, fortunately, to open at home a school in drawing, which not only provided for the family the necessaries of life, but which became, as will be seen later on, the starting point of my mother's career as a teacher of the piano.

Such was the extremely modest course of life in our poor household until the death of my father, which took place on the 4th of May, 1823, in his sixty-fourth year, from inflammation of the lungs. My mother was thus left a widow with two children —my brother, fifteen and a half years old, and myself, five years of age the coming 17th of June.

In dying, my father took with him the livelihood of the family. I will now relate how my mother, by her virile energy and her incomparable tenderness, more than compensated us for the loss of the protection and support of the father who had been taken from us.

There was, at this time, in the *quai Voltaire*, a lithographer, named **Delpech**, whose name was to be seen long afterward on the façade of the house where he lived. Scarcely had my mother become a widow when she hurried to him.

"Delpech," said she, "my husband is no more; I am left alone, with two children to nourish and bring up; from henceforth I must be at once their father and their mother. I will work for them, and I come to ask you two things. How is the lithographic engraving point sharpened, and how is the stone prepared? I will answer for the rest, and I beg you to procure work for me."

Her first care was to announce that she would continue the drawing-school begun by my father, if the parents of the pupils would kindly continue their patronage. With one consent the greatest encouragement and praise were given to the brave initiative of this noble and generous

woman, who, instead of allowing herself to be overcome and buried in
the sorrow of widowhood, raised and
sustained herself through her devotion and tenderness as a mother.

The class in drawing was, therefore, continued and even rapidly aug-
mented by a great number of new
pupils. Furthermore, as my mother,
while well skilled in drawing, was
also an excellent musician, the parents
of her pupils in the former art requested her consent to give their
daughters lessons in music also.

She did not hesitate in taking up
this new resource for meeting the
wants of her little family. The two
branches went well together for a
time, but, as it is unwise to exceed
one's strength in the performance of
a task, it became necessary to choose
between the two arts, and music remained mistress of the situation.

Having known him so little, I have
preserved but few memories of my
father; these are, however, as clear

as if dating from yesterday, and I feel, in retracing them here, an emotion easy to be understood. Among these impressions, I remember particularly his attitude as an attentive reader, seated, with legs crossed, in the corner of the fireplace, wearing glasses, and dressed in long cotton trousers, white striped vest, and cotton cap, such as were usually worn by artists of his time, and which I saw worn many years later by my illustrious and regretted friend, Monsieur Ingres, the director of the Academy of France at Rome. While my father was thus absorbed in reading, I used to lie flat on my stomach on the floor in the middle ·of the room, drawing, with a white crayon on a varnished blackboard, eyes, noses, and mouths, for which he had already traced the copy on the aforesaid board. I see this now as if I were still there, and I was then but four, or four and a half years old at the most. This occupation had for me, I remember,

so great a charm that I have no
doubt if my father had lived I
should have been a painter instead
of a musician, but my mother's profession and the education received
from her during the years of childhood determined the balance in favor
of music.

Soon after the death of my father
in the house — which bore, and still
bears, the number 11, *place Saint-
André-des-Arts* (or, rather, *des Arcs*)—
my mother established herself in
other lodgings not far from there,
number 20, *rue des Grands-Augustins.*
From this time date the first precise
remembrances of my musical impressions. My mother, in nursing me,
had certainly made me imbibe as
much music as milk. She never performed that function without singing, and I can say that I took my first
lessons without knowing it, and without having to give them the attention
so painful to tender years, and so
difficult to obtain from children.

Quite unconsciously I thus early gained a correct idea of intonations and of the intervals they represent; of the first elements of modulation, and of the characteristic difference between the major and minor modes; for one day, even before being able to speak correctly, upon hearing a song in the minor mode, sung by some street musician, probably a mendicant, I exclaimed:

"Mamma, why does he sing in 'do (C)' that cries (*plore*)?"

My ear was, therefore, perfectly trained, and I easily held my place as pupil in a vocal class in which I might even have been a teacher. My mother, proud of seeing her baby able to correct full-grown girls in the matter of reading music (thanks to herself for that), could not resist the desire to show her young pupil to some prominent musician. There was, at this time, a musician named Jadin, whose son and grandson have since made a reputation in painting.

This man Jadin was well known by some songs then in vogue, and filled, if I am not mistaken, the position of accompanist in Choron's celebrated school for sacred music. My mother wrote, begging him to kindly call upon her, and pass judgment upon my musical ability. He came to the house, had me placed with my face turned from him, in a corner of the room that I see yet, seated himself at the piano, and improvised a series of chords and modulations, asking me at each change :

"In what key am I ?"

I made not even one mistake. Jadin was amazed ; my mother was jubilant.

Poor, dear mother; she little thought then that she was developing in her child the germs of a determination which was, but a few years later, to cause her great anxiety on the subject of his future, and upon which already, probably, a great influence had been exerted by my hearing of

Robin des Bois at the *Odéon* theater, where she had taken me when six years old.

Those who read these memoirs will, doubtless, be surprised that I have said nothing concerning my brother. That is because no memories of him were connected with those of my early childhood. It is only after arriving at the age of six years that he takes place in my life and in my remembrance. My brother, Louis-Urbain Gounod, was born December 13, 1807. He was, therefore, ten and a half years older than myself. When about twelve years old, he was sent to the lyceum, at Versailles, where he remained until his eighteenth year. It is from Versailles that dates the first remembrance I have of this excellent brother, who was taken away from me just when I could best appreciate the worth of such a friend.

My father had been appointed by

the king, Louis XVIII., professor of
drawing to the pages of his court.
The king, who was very fond of him,
had authorized our family to occupy,
during the time that we were at Versailles, lodgings situated in the vast
building, No. 6, *rue de la Surintendance,* which extends from the *Place du
Château* to the *rue de l'Orangerie.* Our
apartments, as I still see them, and to
which ascent was made by a number
of stairways of peculiar arrangement,
looked out upon the basin of the
Suisses, and upon the great woods of
Satory. A long corridor, that seemed
to me to extend farther than the eye
could reach, ran past our apartments,
connecting them with those occupied
by the Beaumont family, in which I
found one of the first companions of
my infancy — Édouard Beaumont,
afterward distinguished as a painter.

Édouard's father was a sculptor and
restorer of the statues in the palace
and park of Versailles; it was in this
capacity that he occupied the lodging

next to ours. After the death of my father, in 1823, the privilege was still allowed us of sojourning during the summer vacation in the buildings of the *Surintendance;* this favor was continued under the reign of Charles X., that is to say, until 1830, but was withheld upon the accession of Louis Philippe. My brother, who was, as I have said, in the lyceum at Versailles, passed his vacations with us there.

There was at Versailles an old musician named Rousseau, chapel master of the palace. Rousseau played the violoncello (or bass, as it was then called), and my mother employed him to give lessons on that instrument to my brother, who was gifted with a charming voice, and often sang at the services in the palace chapel. I can not say whether this old father Rousseau played his bass well or ill; but I do remember that my brother gave me the impression of not being very clever on his instrument, and, as I did not understand what it was

to be a beginner, I thought instinct-
ively that if one played an instrument at all, it could not be otherwise
than in tune. The idea that one
could play out of tune never entered
my little head. One day, hearing
my brother practicing his bass in the
next room, and being struck with the
number of more than doubtful passages from which my ear was suffer-
ing, I said to my mother:

"Mamma, why is Urbain's bass so
false?"

I do not remember her reply, but
she must surely have been amused at
the *naïveté* of my question. I have
stated that my brother had a very
fine voice, which fact was later con-
firmed by the opinion of Wartel,
who often sang with him in the
chapel at Versailles, and who, after
having been in Choron's music
school, became a member of the
opera company in the time of Nour-
rit, afterward acquiring a great and
well-earned reputation as a teacher.

In 1825 my mother fell ill, I being
then nearly seven years old. Her
physician, for a long time, was Doctor
Baffos, who was present at my birth,
and who became our family physician after Doctor Halle, by whom he
was recommended. Baffos, seeing in
my presence in the house a super-
addition of fatigue for my mother,
whose days were passed in giving
lessons at home, suggested the idea
of having me taken every morning to
school, and brought home every night
before dinner. The school selected
was that of a Monsieur Boniface, near
the School of Medicine, not far from
the *rue des Grands-Augustins*, where
we were living. This school was
transferred a short time afterward
to the *rue de Condé*, almost opposite the *Odéon* theater. It was there
that I first saw Duprez, who was destined to be one day that well-known
great tenor who shone with such
brilliancy upon the stage of the
Odéon. Duprez, who was nearly nine

years older than I, was then sixteen
or seventeen years of age. He was
a pupil of Choron, and came to the
Boniface school as a vocal teacher.
Seeing that I read music as easily as
one reads a book, and even more
rapidly than I could probably read it
to-day, he took a special liking for
me. Seating me upon his knees,
when my little comrades made mis-
takes, he used to say:

"Come, little man, show them how
to do it."

When, many years later, I recalled
this circumstance to him, so long past
for him as well as for me, he was
greatly struck with it, and said:

"*Comment!* you were the little fellow, then, who sang so well?"

Meanwhile I was approaching the
age when it became necessary to
think of having me begin work under
conditions more serious than were
offered in a house which more re-
sembled a kindergarten than a school.
I was, therefore, placed as a boarder

in the institution of M. Letellier, *rue
de Vaugirard*, at the corner of the
rue Férou. M. Letellier was soon
succeeded by M. de Reusse, whose
house I left at the end of a year to
enter the boarding-school of Hallays-
Dabot, *Place de l'Estrapade*, near the
Panthéon.

I recall M. Hallays-Dabot and his
wife as clearly as if they stood before
me. It would be hard to imagine
treatment more kind, benevolent, and
tender than that I received from
them. I was touched to such an
extent that my first impression was
sufficient to instantly dissipate my
fears, and make me accept with confidence the trial of a new *régime* for
which I felt an insurmountable re-
pugnance. It seemed to me that I
had almost found a father, and that
with him I had nothing to fear.

In fact I have no unpleasant remembrance of the two years passed
in his house. His affection for me
never ceased; I always found him

3

equally just and kind, and when, at
the age of eleven years, it was decided to place me in the *Lycée St.
Louis*, M. Hallays-Dabot gave me a
certificate so flattering that I abstain
from reproducing it. I regard it as
a duty to here make this acknowl-
edgment of what he was to me.

The good recommendations, under
the protection of which I left the
institution of Hallays-Dabot, assisted
in obtaining for me in the *Lycée St.
Louis* a "*quart de bourse.*" I went in
upon these conditions at the close of
the vacation, that is, in the month of
October, 1829. I had just passed my
eleventh birthday.

The principal of the lyceum was
then a priest, the Abbé Ganser, a
man gentle, serious, reserved, and
fatherly with his pupils. I was admitted at once into the class known
as the sixth. I had the good fortune
to have as a teacher, from the beginning, the man whom, without excep-
tion, I loved the most of all during

my school days — my beloved and
venerable master and friend, Adolphe
Régnier, member of the Institute of
France, who was also the preceptor
and has remained the friend of the
Comte de Paris.

I was not a bad pupil, and my
masters generally loved me, but I
was dreadfully thoughtless, and often
brought punishment upon myself for
waste of time; rather, however, during hours of study than in the class.
I have said that I entered the St.
Louis with a *"quart de bourse,"* that is,
with a quarter less to pay than the
usual charge. It was for me to suc-
ceed, little by little, by good reports
of conduct and progress, in relieving
my mother of the expense of the
school, by gradually obtaining the
"*demi bourse*" (half purse), then the
three-quarters, and finally the "*bourse
entière*" (whole purse); and, as I adored
my mother, and my greatest happiness would have been to aid her by
my application to study, it seems as

if this thought ought not to have deserted me for an instant. But, alas! " *Chassez le naturel, il revient au galop!*" And my " *naturel*" galloped very often — far too often!

One day I was punished, I do not know for what shortcoming of inattention, or task unfinished, or lesson unlearned. The punishment seemed to me in excess of the fault, and I protested, which resulted in the additional penalty of being placed in solitary confinement in the cell used for correction of pupils, and where I had to live on bread and water until I had finished an enormous task consisting of, I can not remember, how many lines to write — 500 or 1,000 — an absurdity! When I found myself in prison, oh, then I felt like a criminal! The cry of the Eumenides to Orestes, "He has killed his mother!" could not have been more frightful than the thoughts that assailed me at the moment when they brought me the bread and water of the condemned. I looked at my piece of bread and burst into tears:

"Scoundrel, rascal, wretch!" said I to myself; "it is the labor of your mother that earns for you this piece of bread! Your mother, who will come to see you at the hour of recreation, to whom it will be reported that you are in prison, and who will go home weeping through the streets, without having seen or embraced you. You are a good-for-nothing, and not worthy even to eat this bread!"

And the bread was left untasted.

However, when once more in the usual routine of the school, I worked very well, and, thanks to the prize that I carried off each year, I was in the way of obtaining that "*bourse entière*," the object of all my wishes.

There was at the *Lycée St. Louis* a chapel in which high mass was celebrated every Sunday. The gallery was divided into two parts and ran across the whole width of the chapel. In one of these parts were the organ and the seats reserved for the singers. The chapel master, at the time I entered the lyceum, was Hippolyte Monpou, then employed as accompanist at the Choron school of music, and who has since become known by several melodies and dramatic works that have made his name very popular.

Thanks to the musical education received from my mother from my most tender infancy, I read music at first sight. I had, besides, a very good and true voice, and when I entered the school was presented at once to Monpou, who was astonished at my ability, and immediately appointed me soprano soloist of his little musical band, consisting of two first sopranos, two second sopranos, two tenors, and two basses.

An imprudence of Monpou's caused the loss of my voice. He continued to have me sing during the time of change, in spite of the rest and quiet required by this transformation of

the vocal organs, and after that I
never acquired again the force, sonority, and timbre possessed as a child,
and which are the necessary qualities
of a good voice. Mine remained weak
and husky. But for that accident, I
think I should have made a good
singer.

The revolution of 1830 put an end
to the principalship of the Abbé Ganser. He was replaced by M. Liez, an
old professor of the *Lycée Henry IV.*,
very much devoted to the new *régime*, and a zealous advocate of the
military exercises then being introduced into the schools, and at which
he was always present, standing with
head erect, and right hand slipped *à
la Napoléon* between the buttons of
his redingote, in an attitude of drill-
master or chief of battalion. After
two years, M. Liez was himself replaced by M. Poirson, under whose
directorship began the events that
decided the course of my life.

Among the faults of which I was the most frequently guilty, there was one for which I had a particular weakness. I adored music, and from this passionate fondness, which determined the choice of my career, arose the first tempests that troubled my young existence. Whoever has been brought up in a lyceum knows the festival so dear to schoolboys — that of St. Charlemagne. It is a great banquet, in which all pupils take part who have, since the beginning of the school year, stood once in the first or twice in the second place in the class for composition. This banquet is followed by a leave of absence of two days, which allows the pupils to "*découcher*," that is, to pass one night at home—a pleasure very rare, an indulgence greatly envied by all. The festival falls in the middle of winter. In the year 1831, I had the good fortune to be bidden to this banquet, and, as a reward, my mother promised that I might go in the evening with

my brother to the *Théâtre des Italiens*,
to hear Rossini's **Othello**. Malibran
was playing the part of Desdemona;
Rubini, that of Othello; Lablache,
that of the father. The anticipation
of this pleasure made me wild with
joy and impatience. I remember that
it took away my appetite, so that at
dinner my mother was obliged to say:

"See here! If you do not eat, you
can not go to the *Italiens*."

I immediately set myself to eat
with *resignation*. The dinner hour
was very early, inasmuch as we could
not afford tickets in advance, and it
would be necessary to stand in line to
get places in the parquet at 3 francs,
75 centimes each, which was, even at
that figure, a great outlay for my
poor, dear mother. It was bitter
cold, and my brother and I waited,
with frozen feet, nearly two hours
for the moment so ardently wished
for, and the crowd began to give
way before the ticket office. We
finally entered. Never shall I forget

the impression received at the sight
of that interior, of the curtain, of
the chandeliers. It seemed to me
that I was in a temple, and that
something divine was to be revealed
to me. The solemn moment arrived ;
the three customary raps were given,
and the overture was about to com-
mence. My heart was beating to
burst my breast! That representation was an enchantment, a delirium.
Malibran, Rubini, Lablache, Tambu-
rini (who played Iago), the voices,
the orchestra — all made me literally
wild.

I emerged from the theater thoroughly at variance with the prose of
real life, and completely wrapped up
in that dream of the ideal which had
become my atmosphere, my fixed purpose. I did not close my eyes that
night! I was beset, possessed! I
thought of nothing but of produc-
ing — I also — an Othello! (Alas, my
exercises and translations suffered
severely, and soon showed the effect

of this madness!) I hurried off my work without first writing it in the rough, making at once a copy on finishing paper, so as to be the more quickly rid of it, and to have my undivided time for my favorite occupation — musical composition — which seemed to me the only thing worthy of my attention or thoughts. This was the source of many tears and of great sorrows. My teacher, seeing me scribbling one day on music paper, approached me, and asked for my exercise. I handed him my finished copy.

"And your rough copy?" added he.

As I could not produce it, he took possession of my music paper and tore it into a thousand pieces. I remonstrated; he punished me; I protested, and appealed to the principal. Result — kept in after school, extra task, solitary confinement, etc.

This first persecution, far from curing me, only inflamed more violently

my musical ardor, and I resolved
henceforth to be careful to secure the
enjoyment of my pleasures by the
regular fulfillment of my duties as
a student. At this juncture I determined to address to my mother a
sort of profession of faith, formally
declaring my positive wish to be an
artist. I had, at one time, hesitated
between painting and music; but
finally feeling more inclination to
express my ideas in music, I settled
upon the latter choice.

My mother was completely overcome, as may well be understood.
She had known from experience the
hardships and uncertainty of the life
of an artist, and probably dreaded
for me a second edition of the scarcely
fortunate existence she had shared
with my father. Therefore, she came,
greatly excited, to tell her troubles to
the principal, M. Poirson. He reassured her, saying:

" Do not fear; your son will not be
a musician; he is a good little pupil;

he works hard; his teachers are pleased with him. I will see to it that he is pushed forward to the Normal School. Rest assured, Madame Gounod, he will not be a musician."

My mother went away very much comforted. The principal called me into his office.

"*Eh, bien*," said he to me, "how is this? You wish to be a musician?"

"Yes, sir."

"Ah, but you do not think what that means! To be a musician amounts to nothing in the world."

"What, monsieur! It is nothing to be Mozart? Rossini?"

And I felt while replying to him that my little head of thirteen or fourteen years threw itself backward. Instantly the face of my interlocutor changed expression.

"Ah!" said he, "that is what you think about it. Very well, we will see if you are able to make a musician. I have had a box at the *Italiens* for ten years, and I am a good judge."

He then opened a drawer and, taking out a paper, began to write some verses. This being finished, he handed me the paper, saying:

"Take this away and set it to music."

I was delighted. I left him and went back to my studies. On the way to the class-room I looked over with feverish anxiety the written lines. They were the song of Joseph, *"A peine au sortir de l'enfance . . ."* I knew nothing of Joseph, nor of Méhul. I was neither hindered nor intimidated by any remembrance. It may easily be imagined how little interest I felt for my Latin exercise in this moment of musical intoxication. My song was written during the following recreation hour. I ran in haste with it to the principal.

"What is it, my child?"

"My song is finished."

"What, already?"

"Yes, sir."

"Let us see; sing it to me."

"But, sir, I need a piano for my accompaniment."

Monsieur Poirson had a daughter studying the piano, and I knew there was one in the adjoining room.

"No, no," said he, "that is unnecessary. I do not need a piano."

"But I do, sir, for my chords."

"And where are they, your chords?"

"Here, sir," said I, pointing to my forehead.

"Ah! very well; but it makes no difference to me; sing all the same. I shall understand very well without the chords."

I saw that I had to do without accompaniment, and began; but I was scarcely in the middle of the first part when I perceived the face of my judge softening. This encouraged me, and I commenced to feel that victory was on my side. I went on with confidence, and, when the song was finished, the principal said:

"Now, then; come to the piano."

I triumphed at once; I had all my

weapons in my hands. I recom-
menced my little exercise, and at
the end poor Monsieur Poirson, completely vanquished, with tears in his
eyes, took my head in his two hands
and embracing me, said:

"Go on, my child, with your music."

My dear, sainted mother had acted
prudently; her resistance was a duty
dictated by her solicitude; for, aside
from the danger of giving too easy
consent to my wishes, there was also
the grave responsibility of hindering
my natural vocation. The encouragement given me by M. Poirson
deprived her of the chief support of
her opposition to my plans, and of
the assistance upon which she had
most counted to turn me from them.
The assault had been made, the
siege commenced; it was necessary
to capitulate. She, however, took as
long a time as possible, and fearing
to yield too quickly and too easily to
my wishes, thought of and adopted
the following expedient:

There was then in Paris a German
musician who enjoyed a high reputation as a theorist—Antoine Reicha by
name. Besides his duties as professor
of composition at the Conservatory,
of which Cherubini was then director,
Reicha gave private lessons at home.
My mother thought of putting me in
his hands, and requested of the principal of the lyceum the privilege of
taking me on Sundays, at the time
the school went out for a promenade,
to M. Reicha instead, for the purpose
of beginning the study of harmony,
counterpoint, and fugue — or, in a
word, to learn the preliminaries of
the art of composition. My going,
my lesson, and my return to the
school would take about the same
time as that given to the promenade,
and my regular studies would not
suffer on account of this favor of an
exceptional outing. The principal
consented, and I was taken to M.
Reicha; but, when confiding me to
him, my mother privately said, as she

4

afterward related to me, the following words:

"My dear M. Reicha, I bring you my son, a child who declares that he wishes to devote himself to musical composition. I bring him against my will. An artistic career for him frightens me, for I know with what difficulties it bristles. However, I do not wish to have to reproach myself, nor to give him the right to reproach me in future years for having hindered his ambition, or put obstacles in the way of his happiness. I desire, therefore, to be assured at the outset, that his talents are real and his calling well defined. For this reason I desire to have you put him to a serious test. Place before him difficulties; if he is really called to be an artist, they will not repel him ; he will conquer them. If, on the contrary, he becomes discouraged, I shall know what to do, and shall certainly not allow him to embark in a career, the first difficulties of which he has not the courage to overcome."

Reicha promised to submit me to the *régime* demanded by my mother; and he kept his word, as far as in him lay. As samples of my boyish talent, I took to him several pages of music, containing songs, preludes, bits of waltzes, and what-not else that had passed through my little head. Looking over these, he said to my mother:

"That child already knows a great deal of what I have to teach him; but he does not know that he knows it."

When, at the end of one or two years, I had come to exercises in harmony something more than elementary, to counterpoint of all kinds, to fugues, canons, etc., my mother asked him:

"Well, what do you think?"

"I think, dear madame, that there is no way of tiring him; nothing repels him; everything amuses him, everything interests him; and what pleases me the most is that he always wants to know the 'why.'"

"Very well," said she, "I must be resigned then."

I knew that with my mother there was no trifling. Several times she had said to me:

"You know, if you do not do well — quick, a carriage, and to the notary!"

The notary! That was enough to make me accomplish impossibilities. Furthermore, my reports from school were good, and in spite of the threat suspended over me of making me go twice through the same studies, in order to prolong my time in school, I was careful not to give my teachers the right to consider my musical passion detrimental to my other work. One time, however, I was punished, and that very severely, for not having finished some exercise. The teacher kept me in after school, with a tremendous task — something like 500 verses to copy. I was scrawling away, with that careless rapidity with which one usually does such tasks, when the preceptor approached the table.

After having observed me for some moments in silence, he laid his hand gently upon my shoulder and said :

" That is very badly written—what you are doing there ! "

Raising my head, I replied :

" *Tiens !* perhaps you think it is amusing ! "

" It is tiresome because you are doing it badly ; if you would take more care," added he, quietly, " it would not be so tedious."

This simple remark, so full of good sense, so quiet, and spoken with a tone of patient and persuasive kindness, put such a new light upon the matter, that since that day I do not remember ever to have been negligent or thoughtless at my work. It was a sudden revelation, complete and convincing, of the secret of *attention* and *application*. I set myself again to my task, which was finished with quite a different feeling, and my *ennui* disappeared under the content-

ment and benefit derived from the
good advice just received.

In the meantime, my musical studies were followed with satisfactory
results, becoming more and more
absorbing. A vacation of several
days arrived (that of the New Year),
of which my mother took advantage
to procure for me a pleasure that was
at the same time a great and impressive lesson. They were giving Mozart's *Don Giovanni*, at the *Italiens*,
to a hearing of which she took me
herself; and that heavenly evening
spent with her in a little box on the
fourth floor of that theater is one of
the most memorable and delightful
of my life. I can not say if my
memory is correct, but I think it
was Reicha who advised her to take
me to hear *Don Giovanni*.

Before describing the emotion produced in me by that incomparable
chef-d'œuvre, I ask myself if my pen
can ever transcribe it—I do not say

faithfully, as that would be impossible—but at least in a manner to give some idea of what went on in my mind during those few hours, the charm of which has dominated my life like a luminous apparition, or a kind of vision of revelation.

From the very beginning of the overture I felt myself transported into an absolutely new world, by the solemn and majestic chords of the final scene of the Commandant. I was seized with a freezing terror; and when came the threatening progression over which are unrolled those ascending and descending scales, fatal and inexorable as a sentence of death, I was overcome with such a fright that I hid my face upon my mother's shoulder, and thus enveloped in the double embrace of the beautiful and the terrible, I murmured the following words:

"Oh! mamma, what music! that is, indeed, real music!"

The hearing of Rossini's *Othello*

stirred in me the fibers of musical
instinct, but the effect produced by
Don Juan had quite another significa-
tion, and an entirely different result.
It seemed to me that between these
two kinds of impressions there must
be something analogous to that felt
by a painter in passing directly from
contact with the Venetian masters
to that with Raphael, Leonardo da
Vinci, and Michael Angelo. Rossini
gave me to know the intoxication of
purely musical delight; he charmed
me, delighted my ear. Mozart did
more; to that enjoyment so complete,
from an exclusively musical and emo-
tional point of view, was then added
the profound and penetrating influence of true expression united to perfect beauty. It was, from one end to
the other of the score, a long and
inexpressible delight. The pathetic
tones of the trio at the death of the
Commandant, and of Donna Anna's
lament over the body of her father,
the charming grace of Zerlina, the

supreme and **stately** elegance of
the trio of the Masks, and **of** that
which begins the second act under
Donna Elvira's window — all, finally
(for in this immortal work all must be
mentioned), created for me that beati-
tude one feels only in the presence of
the essentially beautiful things that
hold the admiration of the centuries,
and serve to fix the height of the
esthetic level of perfection **in art.**
This representation counts as one of
the most cherished holiday **gifts of**
my childhood, and later, when I had
won the *prix de Rome*, **it was the**
full score of *Don Juan* **that my dear**
mother gave me as a reward.

That year was, as it happened, particularly favorable to the development of my love of music. During
Holy Week, I heard two concerts by
the concert society of the Conservatory, then directed **by** Habeneck. At
one of these, **Beethoven's** Pastoral
Symphony was played; and at the
other, the symphony with chorus, by

the same master. A new inspiration
was then given to my musical ardor,
and I remember that, while these two
compositions revealed to me the lofty,
bold individuality of this singular
and gigantic genius, I also instinct-
ively recognized in them a manner
of expression similar, in many respects, at least, to that into which the
hearing of *Don Juan* had initiated
me. Something told me that these
two great geniuses, so differently incomparable, had a common country,
and belonged to the same school.

My time at the lyceum was passing
rapidly away. Among the means to
which my mother had recourse to
force me to reflect upon the consequences of my determination, besides
that of counting somewhat on keep-
ing me another year in school, by
having me go twice over the same
studies, she hoped to dissuade me by
declaring that if I held an unlucky
number in the drawing of lots for
the military conscription, she would

be obliged to let me go, being too poor to pay for a substitute. Evidently that was only a subterfuge — the poor woman who had eaten dry bread more than once, so that her children should lack nothing, would have sold her bed rather than be separated from one of us; and, as I was of an age to feel and comprehend how much such a life of devotion and sacrifice imposed upon me in the way of respect and love for my mother, I said to her:

"Very well, dear mamma; say no more about it; I will look out for that; I will exempt myself; I shall have the *prix de Rome*."

I was then in the third class, in which a circumstance had happened that attracted to me special consideration among my comrades. One of our professors, M. Roberge, was particularly fond of Latin poetry. To be clever in Latin verse was to be sure of conquering his good graces.

One day the boys had played some trick upon him, the perpetrator of which would not confess his fault, and no one else was allowed to reveal the secret. On account of this refusal to confess, M. Roberge punished the whole class by depriving us of leave of absence. As the Easter vacation was approaching — a vacation of perhaps three or four days' duration — the punishment promised to be dreadful. Nevertheless, the spirit of our boy-ish solidarity did not falter, and the guilty one remained unknown.

The idea came to me of taking M. Roberge on his weak side, and of trying to unbend him. Saying noth-ing to my comrades, I composed a piece of Latin poetry, the subject of which was the grief of little birds immured in a cage, far from the fields, the woods, the sun, the air, begging for their liberty with piteous cries. It must be that the feeling under the dictation of which my verses were written brought me good luck.

On going into the class-room, I took advantage of a moment when the attention of M. Roberge was turned in another direction, and furtively laid my little composition on his chair. Returning to his seat, he noticed the paper, unfolded it, and began to read. Then he asked:

"Messieurs, who is the author of this poetry?"

I raised my hand.

"It is very good," said he; then added: "Messieurs, I withdraw the refusal of leave of absence; you may thank your comrade, Gounod, whose work has earned you your deliverance."

The civic honors with which I was crowned in return for this amnesty may be imagined!

In due course of time I reached the second class, and found myself again under the instruction of my dear old master of the sixth, Adolphe Régnier. I had, then, among my comrades, Eugène Despois, who be-

came a brilliant pupil of the Normal
School, and afterward a distinguished
humanitarian; Octave Ducrois de
Sixt; and, finally, Albert Delacourtie,
the honorable and intelligent attor-
ney, who has remained one of my
best and most faithful friends. We
four boys occupied between us almost
entirely the "bench of honor." At
Easter I was judged sufficiently advanced to take up rhetoric, which I
studied but three months; and my
progress in other branches having
been so satisfactory, my mother renounced her favorite project of having me go over the ground again. I
left the lyceum at the summer vacation, being then a little more than
seventeen years old.

But I had not finished philosophy,
and my mother did not intend that
any of my studies should be incom-
plete. It was, therefore, arranged to
go on with them at home, so that,
while pursuing my work in composition, I was also preparing for exami-

nation as bachelor of arts, which degree I passed at the end of the year.

I have often regretted not having added that of the baccalaureate of sciences, which would have familiarized me early with a crowd of ideas, the importance of which I appreciated when all too late, and regarding which I have, unfortunately, remained in ignorance. But time was pressing; it was necessary to prepare for winning the *prix de Rome*, to which I aspired, and which was for me a question of life or death for my future. Therefore, there was no time to lose.

Reicha had just died, and I found myself without a teacher. My mother decided to take me to Cherubini, and to ask for my admission into one of the classes in composition at the Conservatory. I carried with me some of my exercises written under Reicha, in order to show Cherubini the degree of my advancement. This, however, was not necessary, as he took only verbal information of my progress, and, when he learned that I had been a pupil of Reicha (who had also taught at the Conservatory), he said to my mother:

"Ah, well! he must now begin again and do it all over in another way. I do not like Reicha's method; he was a German. The young man must now follow the Italian school. I will put him into the class of counterpoint and fugue under my pupil, Halévy."

Now, the Italian school preferred by Cherubini was that great one handed down from Palestrina, just as, for the Germans, the master *par excellence* is Sebastian Bach. Far from discouraging me, this decision delighted me.

"So much the better," said I, repeatedly, to my mother. "I shall only be more thoroughly equipped, having learned from each of these two great schools that which characterizes each. All is for the best."

I went into Halévy's class, Cherubini placing me at the same time,
for lyrical composition, in the hands
of Berton, author of *Montano et Stéphanie*, and of a great number of
works enjoying a well-merited reputation. He was a man of fine mind,
agreeable, delicate in feeling, and a
great admirer of Mozart, the assiduous study of whose works he recommended.

"Read Mozart," repeated he, constantly; "read the *Marriage of Figaro.*"

He was right; this ought to be the
breviary of musicians. Mozart is to
Palestrina and to Bach what the
New Testament is to the Old, both
being considered as parts of one and
the same Bible.

Berton having died about two
months after my entrance into his
class, Cherubini placed me in that of
Le Sueur, the author of *Les Bardes*,
La Caverne, and of several masses

and oratorios; a man serious, reserved, earnest, and devout, with an inspiration sometimes biblical; very much given to sacred subjects; tall, with a face pale as wax, and with the air of an old patriarch. Le Sueur treated me with paternal kindness and tenderness; he was affectionate; he had a warm heart. His instructions, which, unfortunately, lasted only nine or ten months, were very beneficial, and I derived from him ideas, the light and elevation of which insure him an indelible place in my memory and in my grateful affection.

I went over again, under the direction of Halévy, the whole course of counterpoint and fugue; but in spite of my work, with which my master was well satisfied, I never obtained a prize at the Conservatory. My special object was the *grand prix de Rome*, which I was determined to carry off, cost what it might.

I was then going on nineteen years

of age, when I competed for the first
time, and won the second prize. Le
Sueur being dead, I became a pupil
of Paër, who had replaced the former
as teacher of composition. I competed again the following year. My
mother was filled with hope and fear
at the same time, for nothing more
was left me but the *grand prix* or
failure. It was a failure! I was
twenty years old — the age for conscription! But my second prize of
the preceding year gave me one more
chance, a respite of a year, after
which I could enter for the third and
last time into the competition. To
console me for my defeat, my mother
took me for a journey of a month in
Switzerland. She had yet, in spite of
her fifty-eight years, all the freshness
and vigor of a woman of thirty. For
me, also, who, outside of Paris, had
seen only Versailles, Rouen, and
Hâvre, this journey was a series of
enchantments, going from Geneva
by Chamouni to the Oberland, the

Righi, the lakes, and returning by Basel. We went on two mules, setting out early each morning, and retiring late to rest, my mother always being the first one up, and all dressed before I was awake.

I returned to Paris full of new zeal for my work, and determined to finish this time with the *grand prix de Rome.* The date of this competition, so impatiently awaited, came at last. I went into the required seclusion, and carried off the prize! My mother wept; with joy, at first, and then at the thought that this triumph meant speedy separation — and *that* a separation of three years, of which two were to be passed in Rome and the third in Germany. We had never been parted, and the fable of "The Two Pigeons" would come daily to her remembrance.

The artists who won the other grand prizes in the same year with me were: Hébert, for painting,

Gruyère, for sculpture; Le Fuel, for architecture; for engraving on medals, Vauthier, grandson of Galle.

The official distribution of the *prix de Rome* took place near the end of October, at the annual public session of the Institute, during which was performed the cantata of the laureate musician. My brother, who was an architect, had made excellent progress at the School of Fine Arts, as a pupil of Huyot; but, not wishing to leave our mother, and foreseeing, perhaps, that the *grand prix* would take from her, some day, the younger of her two sons, he renounced the competition for Rome, which, in case he had obtained it, would have separated him for five years from that mother whom he adored, and of whom he was the mainstay and support.

But he had received what was called the "departmental prize," awarded to pupils obtaining the greatest number of medals in the course of their studies at the School of Fine Arts. This prize was also announced at the same public session of the Institute, and our mother thus had the happiness of seeing her two sons crowned on the same day.

I have already stated that my brother was a student at the lyceum of Versailles. It was there that he first knew Lefuel, whose father, indeed, was architect of the palace, and who was destined later to make illustrious the name he bore. He found my brother again as a fellow-student in the *atelier* of Huyot, the celebrated architect, one of the designers of the *Arc de Triomphe de l'Étoile;* and from that time forward they were bound together in an indestructible friendship. Lefuel was nearly nine years older than I, and my mother, who loved him as a son, confided me to his care in going to Rome (it may be imagined with how many charges), and I owe it to the memory of this most excellent friend to say that he acquitted himself of his duty with the greatest fidelity and the most watchful care.

Before my departure, an opportunity was offered me of attempting a work, serious enough at any age, and especially so at mine. The chapel master of St. Eustache — Dietsch — who was then director of chorus at the *Opéra*, said to me one day:

"Come, write a mass before starting for Rome; I will have it sung at St. Eustache."

A mass! of mine! at St. Eustache! I thought I was dreaming. I had five months before me, and set myself resolutely to the work. On the day fixed, I was ready, thanks to the assistance of my mother, who had helped me copy the orchestral parts, we not having the means with which to pay a copyist. A mass, with grand orchestra, if you please! I dedicated it, with as much temerity as gratitude, to my beloved and regretted

master, Le Sueur, and directed the
performance of it myself, at St.
Eustache.

My mass was certainly not a remarkable work; it showed the inexperience that might be expected from
a young artist as yet a novice in the
handling of the rich palette of the
orchestra, the acquirement of which
demands such long practice. As to
the value of the musical ideas, considered by themselves, they were
conceived with correct feeling, and
with an instinct truly in harmony
with the sense of the sacred text;
but in the particulars of arrangement and development, there was
much left to be desired. Such as
it was, however, this first attempt
brought me much kind encouragement, with one instance of which I
was especially touched.

At the instant when my mother
and I arrived at home, after the production of the mass, I found waiting
for me at the door of our apart-

ments (we were then living at *No. 8 rue de l'Éperon, rez-de-chaussée*), a messenger with letter in hand. I took it, opened it, and read as follows:

"Bravo! dear young man, whom I knew as a child. All honor to the *Gloria*, to the *Credo*, and especially to the *Sanctus!* It is fine, it is truly religious. Bravo! and thanks; you have rendered me truly happy."

This was from good M. Poirson, my old principal at the *Lycée St. Louis*, and at that time principal of the *Lycée Charlemagne*. He had seen the notice of the production of my mass and hastened, full of interest and anxiety, to hear the first efforts of the young artist to whom he had said, seven years before:

"Go on, my child, with your music."

I was so much affected by his remembrance that I did not take time to enter the house; I made but one bound into the street, leaped into a cab, and arrived at the *Lycée Charlemagne, rue St. Antoine*, where I found my dear old principal, who opened his arms and embraced me with all his heart.

I had then but four days to spend with that mother from whom I was to be separated for three years, and who, through her tears, was preparing everything for the day of my departure. That day approached rapidly.

II.

ITALY.

ON the 5th of December, 1834, Lefuel, Vauthier, and I left Paris at eight o'clock in the evening, by the mail-stage that started from the *rue Jean-Jacques Rousseau*. My brother was the only one to witness our departure. Our first stop was at Lyons. From there we descended the Rhône by Avignon, Arles, etc., to Marseilles. At Marseilles we took a coach.

The coach! how many memories are suggested by the word! Poor, old vehicle!—crushed, ground down, outstripped by the breathless, dizzy speed of the iron wheels of steam—the coach which permitted one to stop, to look, and to peacefully admire the places through which—if, indeed,

not *under* which — the roaring loco-
motive now drags you like a piece
of baggage, and hurls you into space
with the fury of a meteor.

The coach which carried you little
by little, gradually, cautiously, from
one scene to another, instead of that
howitzer on rails that takes you,
sleeping under the sky of Paris, and
throws you, waking, roughly, like a
piece of merchandise, *à l'Anglaise*,
under that of the Orient, without
gradual preparatory transition of
mind or of temperature. Many together, closely packed, and in quick
time, like fish sent by express, so as
to be fresh on arrival!

If progress, that pitiless conqueror,
would, at least, leave life in the vanquished! But no — the coach exists
no longer. I bless it for having been;
it permitted me to enjoy in detail the
admirable route from La Corniche,
which prepares one so well for the
climate and the picturesque beauties
of Italy — Monaco, Mentone, Sestri,

Genoa, Spezzia, Trasimeno, Tuscany, and Pisa, Lucca, Siena, Perugia, Florence — alternating and progressive instruction in nature, which explains the masters, who, in their turn, teach one to observe nature. All this we dwelt upon and enjoyed at our leisure for nearly two months, and on the 27th of January, 1840, entered that Rome which was to be our dwelling place, our instructor, and our initiator into the grand and severe beauties of nature and of art.

The director of the Academy of France, at Rome, then, was Monsieur Ingres, whom my father had known when quite young. Upon our arrival we called upon the director, as was customary, to be personally presented to him. He had scarcely seen me when he exclaimed:

"You are Gounod! *Dieu!* How much you resemble your father!"

And he pronounced upon my father's talent as a draughtsman, his nature, and the charm of his mind and conversation, a eulogy that I was proud to hear from the lips of so eminent an artist, this being for me the most agreeable reception possible.

Each of us having been installed in his allotted lodging — a lodging consisting of one large room, serving for both working and sleeping quarters—my first thought was of the long exile that was to separate me from my mother. I wondered if my work as a student would suffice to help me to endure patiently a separation that my stay in Rome and in Germany would prolong to three years. From my window I perceived in the distance the dome of St. Peters, and involuntarily yielded myself to the melancholy induced by my first experience in solitude, although a building could hardly be called a solitude in which were lodged twenty-eight students, who gathered twice a day, at least, around a common table — in that famous dining-

room where hung the portraits of
all who had studied there since the
foundation of the Academy — and
with which comrades I was of a disposition to soon make acquaintance
and be on good terms.

I must confess it! One of the
reasons that contributed the most to
my loneliness was, undoubtedly, the
impression made upon me by my
arrival in Rome. It was a complete
disappointment. Instead of the city
that I had imagined — majestic in
character, striking in appearance,
magnificent, full of temples, ancient
monuments, and picturesque ruins —
I found myself in a veritable provin-
cial city, ordinary, colorless, and dirty
almost everywhere. My illusions
were completely destroyed, and it
would have taken but little to induce
me to give up my studies, pack my
trunk, and leave post haste for Paris,
there to find again all that I loved.

Of course, Rome contained all that
of which I had dreamed, but not in a

way to strike one at first sight; it must be sought for; one must look here and there, and question, little by little, the sleeping grandeur of the glorious past, bringing it to life again by familiar acquaintance with those silent ruins—the bones of Roman antiquity.

I was too young then, not alone in years, but also in development of mind; I was too much of a child to seize and comprehend at first sight the profound meaning of that grave, austere city, which appeared to me so cold, arid, sad, and taciturn, which speaks in a tone so low as to be understood only by ears trained by silence and meditation. Rome can say what the Holy Scriptures represent God as saying with regard to the soul: "I will allure her, and bring her into the wilderness, and speak comfortably unto her."

Rome is, in herself, so many things, and these things are wrapped in a calm so profound, in a majesty so tranquil and serene, that it is impossible to suspect, at first, the prodigious amount and inexhaustible richness of what she offers. Her past as well as her present, her present as well as her future, make of her the capital, not of a country, but of humanity. Whoever has lived there long knows this very well; and to whatever nation one may belong, whatever may be one's native tongue, Rome speaks a language so universal that none can leave it without feeling as if departing from a native land. Little by little my melancholy gave place to quite another sentiment. I familiarized myself with my surroundings, and emerged from the sort of winding-sheet in which I had been enveloped.

In the meantime I had not been altogether idle. My favorite employment was the reading of Goethe's Faust (in French, of course, as I did not know a word of German). I read, besides, and with great pleasure, the

6

poems of Lamartine. Before thinking of my first composition to be
sent home from Rome, and for which
I had still plenty of time, I busied
myself in writing several melodies,
including *Le Vallon* and *Le Soir*, the
music of which was adapted ten
years later to the prize competition
scene in the first act of my opera,
Sapho, set to the beautiful lines of
my friend and collaborator, Émile
Augier—"*Héro, sur la tour solitaire
. . . .*" I wrote these melodies
within a short time of each other,
almost immediately after my arrival
at the Villa Medici.

Six weeks passed away; my eyes
became accustomed to that city whose
silence had impressed me as a desert.
This silence even began to charm
me, to be a solace, and I found
a particular pleasure in frequenting
the ruins of the Forum, the Palatine
Hill, and the Colosseum, those remains of past grandeur and power
over which has been extended for

centuries the august and pacific
shepherd's crook of the Pastor of
Peoples and the Ruler of Nations.

I had formed the acquaintanceship
and became the friend of an excellent
family, the Desgoffes, who were enjoying the hospitality of Monsieur
and Madame Ingres. Alexander Desgoffe was not one of our fellow-students, but a pupil of Monsieur Ingres,
and a landscape painter of a severe
and noble style. He lived at the
Academy with his wife and daughter,
a charming child of nine years, who
afterward became Madame Paul Flandrin, a woman as admirable in the
capacity of wife and mother as she
was perfect in that of a daughter.
Desgoffe was possessed of a rare
nature ; a heart deep, worthy, devoted, modest ; clear and simple
as a child; faithful and generous.
It was, as may well be supposed, a
great delight to my mother to learn
that I was with kind and excellent
people, who were really fond of me,

whose society afforded some mitiga-
tion of my loneliness, and upon whom
I could depend in case of need for
loving and devoted care.

Our Sunday evenings were usually
passed in the large drawing-room of
the director, to whose apartments
the students were freely admitted on
that day. We always had music.
Monsieur Ingres favored me with his
special friendship. He was a great
lover of music, being passionately
fond of Haydn, Mozart, Beethoven,
and above all, of Gluck, who, by the
nobility and pathos of his style,
seemed to him a Greek, a descendant
of Æschylus, of Sophocles, and Euri-
pides. Monsieur Ingres played the
violin, not as a good performer, much
less a virtuoso, but during his youth
he had played that instrument in the
orchestra of his native city, Montau-
ban, where he assisted in the performance of Gluck's operas. I had,
also read and studied the works of

Gluck. As to Mozart's *Don Juan*, I knew it by heart, and, although I was not a good pianist, I managed to gratify M. Ingres by playing for him the score he adored. I knew equally well the symphonies of Beethoven, for which he had a great admiration. We two often passed a great part of the night entertaining ourselves in this way in the companionship of the great masters, and in a short time I was completely established in the good graces of M. Ingres.

Whoever has not known that gentleman can have but an incorrect and false idea of him. I observed him very closely, familiarly, frequently, and for a long time ; and I can affirm that he was by nature simple and upright, open, candid, and impulsive, with an enthusiasm that sometimes amounted to eloquence. He had the tenderness of a child and the indignation of an apostle ; he had a *naïveté*, a touching sensibility, and a freshness of emotion not met with among

"*poseurs*," with whom some people
have been pleased to number him.

Sincerely humble and modest in
the presence of the masters, but dig-
nified and proud before the self-suf-
ficience and arrogance of ignorance
and pretension, fatherly toward all
the students, whom he considered as
his children, and whom he was careful to treat as such before the visitors
that were received at the Academy,
whoever they might be, such was the
great and noble artist whose valuable
instructions I had the happiness to
receive. I loved him dearly, and I
shall never forget that he expressed
before me some of those luminous
sayings that suffice to light up the
life of any artist who has the good
fortune to comprehend them.

Everyone knows the famous saying of M. Ingres: "Drawing is the
probity of art." He said in my presence another thing which is a whole
synthesis in itself: "There is no
grace without force." It is the truth

that grace and force are complement-
ary to each other in the total of
beauty, force preserving grace from
becoming puerile, and grace prevent-
ing force from becoming brutal. It
is the perfect harmony of these two
elements that marks the height of
art and which constitutes genius.

It has been said, and often mechan-
ically repeated, that M. Ingres was
despotic, intolerant, exclusive; but
he was nothing of all that. If he
asserted himself strongly, it was
because he had strong belief, and
nothing in the world gives more
authority than that. I have never
seen anyone admire more things
than he, simply because he could dis-
cern better than anyone else in
what respect and why a thing was
admirable. But he was prudent; he
knew to what extent the impulses of
the young lead them, without discernment and without method, to be
enamored of, and infatuated with,
certain personal traits of such or such

a master. He knew, also, that these traits, which are the distinctive, personal characteristics of each master, their individual physiognomy by which they are recognized as we recognize each other, are just the very incommunicable peculiarities of their nature ; and that, consequently, it is, in the first place, to say the least, a plagiarism to try to imitate them ; and, furthermore, that this imitation will result fatally in an exaggeration of those qualities, which the imitator will turn into just as many defects. This was the conviction of M. Ingres, for which he was unjustly accused of exclusiveness and intolerance.

The following anecdote will show how honest he was in correcting a wrongly formed first impression, and how little obstinate in his repugnances. I had just let him hear for the first time the admirable scene of Charon and the Shades, in the opera of *Alceste*, not of Gluck, but of Lully.

This first hearing left upon him an impression of stiffness, dryness, and barbarous harshness so painful that he exclaimed :

"That is frightful! it is hideous! it is not music, it is iron!"

I was very careful not to oppose myself, young as I was, to the impetuosity of one for whom I had the greatest respect; I waited to let the storm pass by. Some time afterward he referred to the impression left upon him by this music — an impression already somewhat softened, as it seemed to me — and said :

"Come, let us have that scene from Lully again — Charon and the Shades — I should like to hear it once more."

I sang it again for him; and this time, having become familiar, doubtless, with the simple and severe style of that remarkable portrayal, he was struck with the irony and cunning in the language of Charon, and with the touching lament of those wandering Shades to whom he refused passage

in his boat because they had nothing
with which to pay him. Little by little M. Ingres grew so much attached
to this scene that it became one of
his favorite selections, a repetition of
which he frequently requested.

But his ruling passion was for
Mozart's *Don Juan*, with which we
sometimes remained together until
two o'clock in the morning, at which
point Madame Ingres, ready to drop
with weariness and fatigue, was obliged to close the piano in order to
separate us and make us go, each one
his own way, to bed.

It is true that in the matter of
music, M. Ingres preferred the German school, and did not care much to
talk about Rossini; but he regarded
the *Barber of Seville* as a master-
piece; he had, also, the greatest
admiration for another Italian master
— Cherubini — of whom he left a fine
portrait, and whom Beethoven considered the greatest master of his time,
which is not slight praise, bestowed

by such a man. Moreover, we all have our preferences, and why should M. Ingres not have his? To prefer is not to condemn what one does not prefer.

A particular circumstance favored and increased my intimacy with M. Ingres. I was very fond of drawing, and often carried a sketch-book in my excursions around Rome. One day, returning from one of my expeditions, I found myself at the door of the Academy, face to face with him, also returning at that moment. He noticed the sketch-book under my arm, and said, fixing upon me that searching and luminous look peculiar to him:

"What have you there, under your arm?"

I replied, somewhat confused:

"But — M. Ingres — it is a sketch-book."

"A sketch-book! for what purpose? Do you draw?"

"Oh, no—M. Ingres—that is to say —yes—I draw a little, but so very little.'

"Indeed! ah, come, let me see."

And opening my book his eyes fell upon a small figure of St. Catharine that I had copied that very day from a fresco attributed to Masaccio, in the old basilica of St. Clement, not far from the Colosseum.

"Did you do this?" asked M. Ingres.

"Yes, sir."

"All alone?"

"Yes, sir."

"Ah! but do you know that you draw like your father?"

"Oh! M. Ingres."

Then looking at me seriously, he said:

"You must make me some tracings."

Make tracings for M. Ingres! Perhaps to make them near him, to be illuminated by his rays, to warm myself by his enthusiasm! I was overcome with honor and delight.

Thus it was in fact that, seated by

his side and working at evening by
his lamp, I gave myself up to this
fascinating occupation, so delightful
and at the same time so instructive,
both on account of the study of the
chefs-d'œuvres that passed under the
careful point of my pencil and by all
that I gathered from the conversation of M. Ingres. I made nearly a
hundred sketches for him after en-
gravings of primitive subjects that
had the honor of being in his port-
folio, and of which several were not
less than forty centimètres in height.

One day he said to me:

"If you wish it, I will have you
come back to Rome with the *grand
prix* for painting."

"Oh! M. Ingres," replied I, "change
my career, and begin another? And
then leave my mother again? Oh!
no, no!"

However, as I was in Rome to
devote myself to music rather than
to painting, it was necessary to think

seriously of improving occasions for hearing music. These opportunities were not, indeed, very frequent, but, above all, they ought to have been beneficial and instructive. And to begin with, in the matter of religious music, there was hardly more than a single place where one could go satisfactorily and profitably, and that place was the Sistine Chapel at the Vatican. What went on in the other churches was enough to make one shudder! Outside of the Sistine Chapel, and the one called the Chapel of the Canons in St. Peters, the music was not even good-for-nothing; it was execrable.

One can not imagine a more unsuitable collection of things brought out in the other churches, in the name of the honor of heaven. All the gaudy tinsel of secular music appeared on the stage of these religious masquerades. One hearing of each was sufficient, and after my first experience I was not found there again.

I went, usually, on Sunday to hear High Mass at the Sistine Chapel, frequently accompanied by my friend, Hébert. But the Sistine — to speak of it as it deserves, too much can not be said of the authors of both what one sees and hears there — or rather, of what was once heard there in former days; for, alas! although one may still see the sublime work of Michael Angelo — destructible and already very much changed — it seems that the music of the divine Palestrina no longer resounds under those vaults that the political captivity of the sovereign pontiff has rendered mute, and which mourn eloquently in emptiness the absence of their holy guest.

I went, therefore, as often as possible to the Sistine Chapel. The music there — severe, ascetic, horizontal, and calm as the line of the ocean, monotonous by reason of serenity, ante-sensuous, and, nevertheless, possessing an intensity of contemplation that sometimes amounts to ecstasy—produced at first a strange, almost unpleasant, effect upon me. Whether it was the character of the composition itself, entirely new to me, or the especial sonority of those particular voices, heard for the first time, or, indeed, that attack, firm to harshness, that forcible hammering that gives such strong relief to the various entrances of the voices into a web so full and close, I can not say, but, at any rate, this impression, however strange it might have been, did not displease me. I went the second time, and still again, and finished by not being able to do without it.

There are works that must be seen or heard in the places for which they were created. The Sistine Chapel is one of these exceptional places, unique of its kind in the world. The colossal genius who decorated its vaulted ceiling and the wall of the altar with his matchless concep-

tions of the story of Genesis and of
the Last Judgment, the painter of
prophets, with whom he seemed to
be on an equality, will, doubtless,
never have his equal, no more than
Homer or Phidias. Men of this
stamp and stature are not seen twice
upon the earth; they are syntheses,
they embrace a whole world, they
exhaust it, they complete it, and
what they have said no one can
repeat after them. The music of
Palestrina seems to be a translation
in song of the vast poem of Michael
Angelo, and I am inclined to think
that these two masters explain and
illustrate each other in the same
light, the spectator developing the
listener, and reciprocally, so that,
finally, one is tempted to ask if the Sistine Chapel — painting and music — is
not the product of one and the same
inspiration. Music and painting are
there found in a union so perfect
and sublime that it seems as if the
whole were the twofold expression

7

of one and the same thought, the double voice of one and the same hymn. It might be said that what one hears is the echo of what one sees.

There are, in fact, between the works of Michael Angelo and of Palestrina such analogies, such a similarity of ideas, that it is very difficult not to conclude that these two privileged beings were possessed of the same combination of qualities, and I was about to say, of virtues. In both the same simplicity, the same modesty in the employment of means, the same indifference to effect, the same disdain of seductive attractions. One feels that the material agent, the hand, counts for nothing, and that the soul alone, unalterably fixed upon a higher world, strives only to express in an humble and subordinate form the sublimity of its contemplations. There is nothing, even to the general, uniform tone in which this painting and this music are enveloped, which does not seem created with a sort of voluntary renouncement of all colors. The art of these two men is, so to speak, a sacrament, where the visible sign is no more than a veil thrown over the divine and living reality. Thus, neither one nor the other of these two grand masters fascinates at first. In everything else it is the exterior that attracts; but here, not so; one must penetrate beyond the visible and the sensual.

The hearing of a work of Palestrina produces something analogous to the reading of one of the grand pages of Bossuet. Nothing is noticed as you go along, but at the end of the road you find yourself carried to prodigious heights; the language, docile and faithful servant of the thought, has not turned you from your course nor stopped you in its own interest; and you arrive at the summit without rude shock, without turning from the way, and without accident, conducted by a mysterious guide who has concealed from you both himself and his methods. It is this absence of visible means, of worldly artifices, of vain coquetry, that renders the highest works absolutely inimitable. To attain to the same degree of perfection requires the same spirit by which they were conceived, and the same raptures by which they were dictated.

As to the immense, gigantic work of Michael Angelo, what can I say? What he has spread out, lavished, heaped up in genius—not only as a painter, but as a poet—upon the walls of the Sistine Chapel, is prodigious. What a powerful assemblage of facts and of personages that one comprising and symbolizing the principal history, the essential history, of our race! What a conception that double line of prophets and sibyls, whose far-seeing vision pierces intuitively the veil of the future and carries across the ages the Spirit before whom all things are revealed!

What a book is that vaulted ceiling showing the first history of man, associated in idea, through the colossal figure of the prophet Jonah escaped from the bowels of the whale, with the triumph of the other Jonah delivered by his own power from the shadows of the tomb, and conqueror over death! What a radiant and sublime hosanna that legion of angels turning and winding in a transport of enthusiasm, so to speak, around the sacred instruments of the Passion, which they are carrying through the luminous space to the heights of celestial glory, whilst in the lower abysses of the picture the figures of the doomed stand forth, mournful and despairing, in the last livid lights of a day that seems to say farewell to them forever!

And upon the vaulted ceiling itself, what an eloquent and pathetic representation of the first hours of our first parents! What a revelation that imposing gesture of the creative

act which endows the still inanimate
statue of the first man with the " living soul," which places him in conscious relationship with the author of
his being! What spiritual power is
suggested by that empty space, so
narrow and yet so significant, left by
the painter between the creating
finger and the creature, as if he meant
to say that the divine will knows
neither distance nor obstacle in passing over to and reaching its object,
and that for God to will and to
create are but one and the same
operation ; or, as expressed in the
language of theology, an act of simple volition.

What grace in that submissive
attitude of the first woman, when,
evolved from the depths of Adam's
slumber, she finds herself in the
presence of her Creator and her
Father! How wonderful that im-
pulse of filial feeling and expansive
gratitude with which she bows herself beneath the hand that receives

and blesses her with calm and sovereign tenderness!

But if one were to stop at each step, no more could be done than to merely skim over the surface of this wonderful poem, the extent of which is confusing to the mind. It can almost be said of this most remarkable embodiment of pictures from the Bible, that it is the Bible of painting. Ah! if the young could but understand what there is of education for their intelligence and of spiritual nourishment for future years in this sanctuary of the Sistine Chapel, they would spend entire days there, and neither the calls of self-interest nor the desire for fame could take hold of characters molded in so high a school of fervor and meditation.

Besides profiting by this grand tradition of sacred music maintained in the services of the pontifical chapel, I was also expected, as a student, to make a study of dramatic music. The

repertoire of the theater in Rome, at
this time, was almost entirely made
up of the operas of Bellini, Donizetti,
and Mercadante, all of them works
which, in spite of their individual
characteristics and the occasional
personal inspiration of their authors,
were, by the *ensemble* of means employed, by their conventional style,
and by certain forms, degenerated
into formulas, so many plants trained
around the robust Rossinian trunk,
of which they had neither the vitality
nor the majesty, and which seemed
to disappear under the momentary
brilliancy of their ephemeral foliage.
There was, besides, no musical profit
to be obtained from these representations, which, in point of execution,
were much inferior to those at the
Théâtre des Italiens in Paris, where
the same works were interpreted by
the best of contemporary artists.

The stage-mounting itself was
sometimes even grotesque. I remember being once at the Apollo Theater

in Rome during a representation of
Norma, in which the Roman soldiers
wore the short coat and helmet of a
fireman, and butter-colored nankeen
trousers, with cherry-red bands! It
was positively comical, and one might
have believed himself at a Punch and
Judy show.

I went, therefore, but rarely to the
theater, finding it more profitable to
study at home the scores of my beloved favorite masters, Gluck's *Iphi-
genia*, Lully's *Alceste*, Mozart's *Don
Juan*, and Rossini's *William Tell*.

Besides the hours of companionship passed with M. Ingres during
that famous time of the tracings, I
had the good fortune to be allowed
to see him at work in his studio, and it
may be believed that I took good care
to profit by such a favor. While he
painted, I read to him, and, as one
may well suppose, I interrupted myself more than once to watch him
paint. It was thus that I saw him

correct and finish his exquisite picture, *La Stratonice*, since become the
property of the Duke of Orleans,
and his *Vierge à l'Hostie*, destined
for the gallery of Count Demidoff.
There is an interesting circumstance
connected with the history of this
last painting, to which I was witness.

In the original composition the
foreground was not occupied with the
ciborium surmounted by the Sacred
Host, but by an admirable figure of
the infant Jesus lying asleep, his
head reposing upon a cushion, one
tassel of which he was holding in his
little hand, and with which he seemed
to be still·playing. There was something exquisite about it—so it seemed
to me, at least—in the grace of design,
the beauty of the painting, and the
childish abandon of the position of
the charming little body, so radiant
and dimpled. M. Ingres himself
seemed well satisfied, and when I
left him as the fading light obliged
him to suspend work, he was de-

lighted with the result of his day's labor.

In the afternoon of the next day I ascended again to his studio. No more infant Jesus! The figure had disappeared, scraped off entirely with a palette knife, not a trace of it remaining.

"Ah! M. Ingres!" cried I, in consternation.

And he, with a triumphant, determined air, replied:

"*Mon Dieu*, yes!" And then again, with stronger emphasis, "Yes!"

The splendor of the divine symbol had just appeared to him superior to the radiant human reality, and, therefore, more worthy of the homage of the Virgin adoring her Son. He did not hesitate to sacrifice a work of art to a truth. It is by such noble preferences, by such disinterested severity, that we recognize the men whose privilege and legitimate reward it is to enjoy that indisputable authority which classes them among the guides and teachers of other men.

The company of students at the Academy of France at Rome, in my time, counted among its members many young artists, of whom several have since become celebrated: Lefuel, Hébert, Ballu the architect — all three to-day members of the Institute.

And others who either distinguished themselves or were removed by premature death, with their country's hopes full upon them: Papity, the painter; Octave Blanchard, Buttura, Lebouy, Brisset, Pils, the sculptors Diébolt and Godde; the musicians Georges Bousquet, Aimé Maillart — all were offshoots of that school so much decried, which, after Hippolyte Flandrin and Ambroise Thomas, produced Cabanel, Victor Massé, Guillaume, Cavelier, Georges Bizet, Baudry, Massenet, and many other eminent artists whose names

should be added to this already
respectable list.

The students were often invited to
the *soirées* of the French ambassador.
It was there that I saw for the first
time, Gaston de Ségur, then attaché
of legation, and since become the
venerable bishop known to all the
world, and whom I have the honor to
count among my tenderest and most
faithful friends.

To the sojourn in Rome, which
was our regular and permanent residence, were added the excursions
authorized into other parts of Italy.

I shall never forget the impression
made upon me by Naples, the first
time I arrived there, with my
comrade, Georges Bousquet, now
deceased, who had won the *grand
prix* for music the preceding year.
We made the journey with the Marquis Amédée de Pastoret, who wrote
the words of the cantata with which
I gained the same prize for music.

That enchanting climate, which
gives a foretaste and conception of
the sky of Greece; that bay, blue as
a sapphire, encircled in a belt of
islands, and mountains whose slopes
and summits take at sunset that inces-
santly changing scale of magic tints
which eclipse the richest velvet and
the most glittering gems—all produced upon me the effect of a dream
or a fairy tale. The environs—those
wonderful places called Vesuvius,
Portici, Castellamare, Herculaneum,
Sorrento, Pompeii, the islands of
Ischia and of Capri, Posilipo, Amalfi,
Salerno, and finally Pæstum, with
its admirable Doric temples, once
washed by the blue waves of the
Mediterranean—seemed to me a veritable vision. It was quite the contrary of Rome; it was instantaneous
delight.

If to these attractions be added
the interest which attaches to a visit
to the Museum of Naples — a treasure-
house unique in its way by reason of

the masterpieces of ancient art contained therein, the greater part of
which were brought to light in the
excavations of Pompeii, Herculaneum, Nola, and other cities buried
eighteen hundred centuries under
the eruptions of Vesuvius — one may
easily understand how great must be
the attracting power of such a city,
and how much delight there waits
upon an artist.

Three times during my stay in
Rome I had the pleasure of visiting
Naples, and among the deepest and
most vivid impressions brought from
there, I place in the first rank the
wonderful island of Capri, so rugged
and at the same time so smiling,
thanks to the contrast between its
steep cliffs and green declivities.

It was in summer that I visited
Capri for the first time. The sun
was shining fiercely and the heat
was torrid. During the day it was
necessary either to immure one's
self in a room, in the effort to win

from obscurity a little coolness and sleep, or to plunge into the sea and there pass a part of the day, which I used to do with great delight. But the most difficult thing to imagine is the splendor of the nights in that climate and at that season of the year. The vault of heaven literally palpitates with stars; one might call it another ocean whose waves are of light, so perceptibly does the scintillation of the stars fill and cause to vibrate the infinite space. During the two weeks of my sojourn there I often went to listen to the living silence of those phosphorescent nights, many of which I passed entirely, seated upon the summit of some steep rock, my eyes fixed upon the horizon, and sometimes rolling down the perpendicular height a big stone, to the sound of which I listened until it reached the sea and buried itself there in a spray of foam. At long intervals some solitary bird uttered a mournful note, which carried

my mind toward those weird preci-
pices, the impression of whose terrors
has been so wonderfully rendered
by Weber's genius, in the immortal
scene of the casting of the bullets, in
his opera of *Der Freischütz.*

The first idea of the *Walpurgis
Night* in my opera based on Goethe's
Faust came to me in one of these
nocturnal excursions. This poem
was never out of my possession; I
carried a copy of it everywhere, and
recorded in scattered notes the different ideas that might be of use some
day when I should attempt this subject as an opera — an undertaking
which was not realized until seventeen years later.

But the time came to travel again
the road to Rome, and to reënter the
Academy. However agreeable and
seductive my stay in Naples, I could
not have remained there without
feeling, at the end of a certain time,
the need of a return to Rome.

Something like homesickness took possession of me, and 1 departed without sadness from the place to which I was indebted for so many delightful hours.

Notwithstanding its splendor and prestige, Naples is, after all, a noisy, dirty, tumultuous, excitable, shriek-ing, screaming city. The people struggle, wrangle, quarrel, banter, and dispute from morning to night and from night to morning, upon the quays, where there is neither silence nor repose. Altercation is their normal condition, and one is there besieged, importuned, beset by the indefatigable onslaught of the "*fac-chini*," sellers of merchandise, coach-men, and boatmen, who, for a trifle, would take you by force, and bid among themselves for the lowest price.*

Having returned to Rome, I set

---

*See in appendix the letter from Gounod to Lefuel, dated July 14, 1840.

myself again to work. This was in
the autumn of 1840. My mother, in
spite of her duties as a teacher,
which, during the week occupied her
from morning until night, still found
time to keep up a large part of our
correspondence. It was only by
robbing herself of sleep that she
could find the time thus consecrated
to me by her tender and constant
solicitude. I received from her letters, the length of which indicated
the great amount of rest of which
she must have deprived herself in
order to write them. I knew that
she was always up at five o'clock
in the morning, to be ready to
receive her first pupil, who came
at six; and that, very often, her
breakfast hour was sacrificed to
a lesson, during which she took no
other nourishment than soup, or,
perhaps, a piece of bread, with a glass
of wine. I knew, also, that this business lasted until six o'clock in the
evening; that after dinner she had

to busy herself with the thousand cares of a housekeeper; that she had, moreover, to write to many others besides me; and that, still further, being a charitable woman, she often worked with her own hands to clothe the poor whom she visited. Finally, she did a thousand things that one could not accomplish without order and economy in the disposal of time. She was endowed in the highest degree with those two essential and fundamental qualities upon which rests every useful and well-filled life. For example, she had erased from her programme the useless function of the "social call," which consists in wasting one's time from Monday to Saturday in going to visit others, only to make them waste theirs, also, in an effort to "kill" the time of which everyone dies with *ennui* who does not use it for the serious purposes of life. Thus she brought us up according to short but far-reaching maxims like the following, thrown out in passing, with the laconicism of people who have no time to be talkative: "Whoever makes no useless outlay always finds the means for necessary expenses;" "Whoever loses not a minute has always the time to do what he ought to do."

One of the friends of our family used to say to me: "In my opinion, your mother is not only one miracle, but two; I do not know where she finds the time for what she does, nor the money that she gives away." . The more she had to do, the more she did. This is the reverse of a charming saying of Émile Augier, but which signifies the same thing: "I have been so very much unoccupied that I have not had time to do anything."

From time to time my dear, good brother slipped into my mother's letters kind words and judicious counsels addressed to me. I had great need of them, for I must admit that stability of judgment has never been my strong point, and a *weakness* is very *strong* when reason does not serve as a counterweight. Alas! I profited badly by all that, and I make of it my *meâ culpâ*

There is in Rome, in the Corso, a church called *St. Louis des Français*, the services of which are conducted by French priests. Every year, at the festival of the king, Louis Philippe, that is to say, on the 1st of May, they used to celebrate in this church a high mass composed by the music student then at the Academy by right of the *grand prix*. The year of my arrival there, the mass performed (with orchestra) was by my comrade, Georges Bousquet. The following year it was my turn. Fearing that, with my duties as a student, I might not have the time to accomplish a work of this importance, my mother sent me my mass of St. Eustache, entirely copied anew by her own hand from the manuscript of my orchestral score, and from which she did not wish to part, nor to risk its transportation through the mail.

My feelings upon receiving at Rome this new proof of maternal patience and tenderness may easily be imagined. But I did not make the use of it intended by my mother. It seemed to me more worthy of a conscientious artist to try to do better than that (which was not difficult), and I bravely continued my work upon the new mass already commenced for the king's fête. I composed it and directed its execution myself.* This work brought me good luck. Besides the very indulgent congratulations received on its account, I owe to it my appointment as honorary chapel master for life of the church of *St. Louis des Français* at Rome. I hardly thought then that I should have occasion the following year, in Ger-

*Regarding a repetition of this mass, see in appendix, letter of Gounod to Lefuel, dated April 4, 1841.

many, to bring it out again and to direct it myself. It will be seen later in what way I was affected by the consequences and advantages of this second performance.

The longer my stay in Rome, the more deeply attached I became to that city, so mysteriously attractive, so incomparably peaceful. After the crenelated, volcanic, bounding lines of the crater of Naples, the placid, solemn, silent lines of the Campagna of Rome, surrounded by the Alban Mountains, the hills of Latium, and the Sabine range, the majestic Mount Gennaro, Mount Soracte, the mountains of Viterbo, Mount Mario, Mount Janiculus, gave me the sweet and serene impression of a cloister under the open sky.

One of the places of my preference in the environs of Rome was the village of Nemi, with its lake surrounded with thick woods of a splendid luxuriance, and at the bottom of

which is seen a vast crater. To make
the tour of this lake by the upper
road is one of the most delightful
trips of which it is possible to dream.
Taken on a beautiful day, ended with
such a sunset as it was once my privilege to witness, while viewing the sea
from the heights of Genzano, it is a
charming and ineffaceable memory.

The environs of Rome abound in
admirable locations, affording the
traveler and the artist an inexhaustible series of excursions — Tivoli,
Subiaco, Frascati, Albano, Ariccia,
and a thousand other places explored
many times by landscape painters, to
say nothing of the Tiber, the banks
of which have a character so noble
and majestic.

Among the works of art to be
found only in Rome, why should I
pass by in silence, in these memoirs
of my youth, a work of unrivaled
beauty, which divides with the Sistine
Chapel the interest and the glory of

the Vatican ? I mean those immortal
paintings composing the collections
found in *"Le Loggie"* and *"Le Stanze"*
of Raphael. Among the latter, in the
" Stanza della Segnatura," are to be
seen those immortal pages of the
"School of Athens " and the " Dispute
About the Holy Sacrament."

These two *chef-d'œuvres*, among so
many others due to the brush of this
celebrated artist, have carried so high
the standard of beauty that it seems
impossible ever to surpass them. But,
nevertheless, such is the irresistible
ascendency of genius, that this man
whose name the centuries have placed
at the summit of glory, this Raphael,
in fact, was troubled by Michael
Angelo. He felt the embrace of that
Titan ; he bent under the might of
that Colossus, and his last works show
traces of homage rendered to the
mighty inspiration of that great and
powerful brain, which surpassed all
human proportions.

Raphael is the *first*, Michael

Angelo is the *only*. With Raphael, force dilates and expands itself into grace; with Michael Angelo, it is grace which seems, on the contrary, to discipline and control force. Raphael charms and fascinates; Michael Angelo fascinates and crushes. One is the painter of the terrestrial paradise, but the other seems to pierce with the eye of an eagle, like the prisoner of Patmos, into the burning realm of seraphim and archangels.

It may be said that these two great evangelists of art were placed near each other in the fullness of the esthetic age, in order that he who had received the gift of serene and perfect beauty might be to the sight a restful protection from the dazzling splendors revealed to the singer of the Apocalypse.

A detailed analysis of the innumerable masterpieces of art in Rome would be beyond the scope of these memoirs, in which my main object is

to retrace the principal circumstances
of my youth and artistic career.

It was in the winter of 1840-1841
that I had the pleasure of seeing and
hearing, for the first time, Pauline
Garcia, sister of Malibran, and who
had just married Louis Viardot, then
director of the *Théâtre des Italiens* in
Paris. She was then only eighteen
years old, and her early appearances
at the above-named theater were remarkable events. She was taking her
wedding tour with her husband, and
I had the honor and pleasure of playing her accompaniment to the celebrated and immortal air from *Robin
des Bois*, when she sang in the
drawing-room of the Academy. I
was amazed at the wonderful talent
of that *child*, who promised to be, and
who did become, later, an illustrious
woman. I did not see her again until
ten years afterward. Strange circumstance! When twelve years old,
I had heard Malibran in Rossini's

Othello, and had **carried** away from that representation the dream of consecrating myself to musical art. At twenty-two years of age I made the acquaintance of Malibran's sister, Madame Viardot, for whom I was, when thirty-two years old, to write the rôle of *Sapho*, which she created in 1851, upon the stage of the *Odéon* theater, with most brilliant success.

The same winter I had the pleasure, also, of making the acquaintance of Fanny Henzel, sister of Mendelssohn. She was passing the winter in Rome, with her husband — painter to the king of Prussia — and her son, who was still quite a child. Madame Henzel was a musician beyond comparison, a remarkable pianist, and a woman of superior mind; small and thin in person, but with an energy that showed itself in her deep eyes and in her fiery glance. She was gifted with rare ability as a composer, and to her are due several of the *Songs Without Words* pub-

lished in the piano collection under
her brother's name. Monsieur and
Madame Henzel came to the
Academy on Sunday evenings. She
used to place herself at the piano
with the good grace and simplicity
of those who make music because
they love it, and, thanks to her fine
talent and prodigious memory, I was
brought to the knowledge of a mass
of the *chefs-d'œuvres* of German music,
of which I was completely ignorant
at that time; among others, a number
of pieces by Sebastian Bach — sona-
tas, concertos, fugues and preludes —
and several of Mendelssohn's compositions, which were, also, a revelation to me from an unknown world.
Monsieur and Madame Henzel left
Rome to return to Berlin, where I
was to see them again two years
later.

Before leaving the Academy, M.
Ingres presented me with a souvenir,
doubly precious, both as an evidence
of his affection and as a production

of his talent. He painted my portrait in crayon, representing me seated at the piano and having before me Mozart's *Don Juan.*

I deeply realized the void that would be caused by his departure, and to what an extent I should miss the salutary influence of a master whose faith was so firm, whose ardor so communicable, and whose teachings so sure and elevated. There is, in the arts, something besides technical excellence and special ability, or the knowledge and possession, however perfect, of methods. *All that* is good, and even absolutely necessary, but it constitutes only the material part of the artist, the covering and body of any particularly designated art. In all arts there is something which belongs exclusively to none, and which is common to all, above all, and without which they are nothing more than mere professions. This something — which is invisible, but which is the soul and life — is art.

Art is one of the three great trans-
formations that realities undergo in
contact with the human mind, according as it considers them in the ideal
and governing light of one of the
three great aspects — the good, the
true, and the beautiful. Art is no
more a mere dream than it is a mere
copy; it is neither the ideal alone
nor the real alone; it is like man
himself, the meeting, the combination of the two. It is unity in dual-
ity; judged by the ideal alone, it is
above us; by the real alone, it is
below us. Morality is the humaniza-
tion, the incarnation of the good;
science, that of the true; art, that of
the beautiful.

It was to this apostolate of the
beautiful that M. Ingres belonged; it
was his life. This was perceptible in
his discourses as well as in his works,
and even more, perhaps, in the latter
than in the former, to such a degree are men of *faith* also men of
desire, and so far does the effort of

aspiration carry them beyond the beaten path. From this height he threw as much light upon a musician as upon a painter, and revealed to all the common ground of the highest truths. In giving me to understand what is art in general, he taught me more regarding my special art than could have done any number of purely technical masters.

However little I may have gathered from this valuable intercourse, this little sufficed to leave upon me an impression never to be effaced, and a remembrance of him which almost took the place of his actual presence.

In the month of April, 1841, M. Ingres was replaced by M. Schnetz, a distinguished painter, who owed his success and his popularity principally to qualities of sentiment and expression. He was amiable, affectionate, of great natural intelligence, very cordial with the students, jovial, and with a gentle and benevolent face, in

9

spite of a thick hedge of black eyebrows that went to meet an abundant growth of hair nearly covering his whole forehead. M. Schnetz was, above all, of the type called a *bon enfant*. I passed the second and last year of my stay in Rome under his direction.

M. Schnetz had for that city a great predilection, which was specially favored by circumstances. He was three times appointed director of the Academy, where he left the most favorable impression.

My time of residence in Rome was to expire with the year 1841, but I had not the force to take myself away, and, with the consent of the director, prolonged my stay nearly five months beyond the regulation period, leaving only at the last extremity, and having no more than just enough means for my journey to Vienna, where I was to receive the first half of my third year's pension.

I shall not attempt to describe my

sorrow when the time came to say farewell to that Academy, to those dear comrades, to that Rome where I felt that I had taken root. My fellow-students accompanied me as far as the Ponte Molle, and after having embraced them, I mounted the coach which was to *tear* me away —yes, that is, indeed, the word— from those two blessed, happy years in the Promised Land. If, at least, I could have gone directly to see my dear mother and my good brother, this departure would have cost me less pain; but I was going to be alone in a country where I knew no one, and of the language of which I was ignorant, and this perspective could not fail to appear cold and dreary to me. As long as the route allowed, my eyes remained fixed upon the cupola of St. Peter's, that summit of Rome and center of the whole world. When the hills concealed it entirely from my sight, I fell into a deep reverie and wept like a child.

III.

LEAVING Rome for Germany, my
way naturally lay through Florence
and the north of Italy, turning on
the right toward Ferrara, Padua,
Venice, and Trieste.

I stopped in Florence, of which
city I will not attempt to name in
detail the objects of interest, for,
like Rome, it is inexhaustible in
works of art. The Uffizi Gallery,
with its admirable *Tribuna*—a veritable shrine of relics of the beautiful
—the Pitti Palace, the Academy, the
convents, all overflow with *chefs-
d'œuvres*. But there, also, in that
delightful city of Florence, the
scepter is in the hand of Michael
Angelo, who dominates everything
from the height of the marvelous

(132)

and impressive Chapel of the Medici. There, as in Rome, his genius has left its unique, sovereign, unrivaled imprint.

Wherever one meets Michael Angelo, he commands serious attention. As soon as he speaks, one feels that all else must be still, and this supreme authority of silence is, perhaps, nowhere exercised with more force than in this awe-inspiring crypt of the Chapel of the Medici. What a grand conception is that of the *Pensieroso*, mute sentinel seeming to guard the dead and waiting immovably the trumpet-call of the judgment! What repose and grace in that figure of Night, or rather of the Peace of Sleep, forming a companion piece to the robust figure of Day, lying extended, and as if enchained, until the dawn of the last of days! It is by the profound meaning, by the choice of attitude, at once ideal and natural, that Michael Angelo raises himself everywhere to that intensity of expression which is the distinguishing characteristic of his powerful individuality. The amplitude of his figures naturally results from the grandeur of his conceptions — a great river-bed hollowed out by the majestic stream of his thoughts — and it is this which forcibly condemns as pompous and inflated all imitations of forms that his genius alone could perfect, because he only could fill and vivify them.

But I am on my way to Germany, where time and money urge me to arrive, and I must glide rapidly over Florence and the pleasant memories brought away from there. I passed through the deserted Ferrara, and stopped at Padua a day or two to visit the fine frescoes of Giotto and Mantegna.

My stay in Italy had given me a knowledge of the three great cities that are the principal birthplaces of art in that specially favored country: Rome, Florence, and Naples—Rome, the city of the soul; Florence, the city of the intelligence; Naples, the city of pleasure and of light, of intoxication and of dazzling glory.

It remained for me to know a fourth, which has held, also, a great and glorious place in the history of the arts, and to whose natural features her geographical situation has given a character unique and exceptional in the world—Venice.

Venice, joyous and sad, light and somber, rosy and livid, coquettish and sinister, a constant contrast, a strange combination of the most opposite impressions, a pearl in a cesspool!

Venice is an enchantress; she is the home of painters of radiance; she has invested art with sunlight. Contrary to Rome, which waits for you, solicits you slowly, and conquers you invincibly and forever, Venice seizes you by the senses and fasci-

nates you instantly. Rome is serene
and pacifying, Venice is exhilarating
and disquieting ; but the exhilaration
that she induces is mixed (at least
it was for me) with an indefinable
melancholy — a feeling of captivity.
Was it the thought of the dark
dramas of which she has been the
theater, and to which her location
seems to have predestined her? It
may be; at any rate, a long sojourn
in this sort of amphibious necrop-
olis would not seem possible without ending by feeling one's self
asphyxiated and swallowed up in
spleen. Those still-standing waters,
washing in gloomy silence the foun-
dations of the old palaces; that dark,
shadowy surface, from the depths
under which one thinks he hears
the groans of some illustrious victim,
make of Venice a kind of capital of
Terror ; she has retained the impression of the Sinister. And yet,
under fine sunlight, what magic
in the Grand Canal! What reflec-

tions from those lagoons, when the wave transforms itself into light! What power of brilliancy in those old remains of ancient splendor, which seem to contend among themselves for the favors of the sky, and to ask its aid against the abyss into which they are falling, day by day, finally to disappear forever!

Rome invites to meditation, Venice to dissipation; Rome is the grand Latin ancestor, who, through the channel of conquest, will spread over the world the catholicity of language — prelude and means to a catholicity, vaster and of deeper meaning. Venice is an Oriental, not of the Greek, but of the Byzantine type; more suggestive of satraps than of pontiffs, and of Asiatic luxury than of the solemnities of Athens or of Rome.

There is nothing there, even to that marvel of the Church of St. Mark, which does not resemble rather a mosque than a basilica, or cathedral, and which does not appeal more to the imagination than to the sentiment or the soul. The magnificence of those mosaics, and of that gold, the dull, subtly changing colored lights from which stream from the height of the dome down to the foundation, is something absolutely unparalleled in the world. I know of nothing equal to it in vigor of tone and strength of effect.

Venice is a passion, not a love. I was seduced upon entering, but when I left, it was not with that sense of tearing myself away as when bidding farewell to Rome, the strength of which feeling shows the force of the ties that bind.

Naples is a smile, a reflection from Greece ; her horizon drowned in purple and azure, her blue sky reflecting itself in the sapphire waves; all, even to her ancient name of *Parthenope*, plunge you again into that brilliant civilization to which nature set such charming surroundings. Quite different is the smile of Venice, at the same time caressing and perfidious; it is like a feast above a dungeon-trap. It was for this reason, undoubtedly, that, in spite of her masterpieces and the magic with which she is enveloped, I had at departure, and without knowing why, a feeling of deliverance rather than of regret.

From Venice my route was by steamboat to Trieste, where I took the *diligence* for Graetz. On the way I visited the curious and superb grottoes of stalactites at Adelberg — real subterranean cathedrals. I crossed the Carinthian Mountains, of whose jagged silhouette I made a sketch as we went along. I arrived at Graetz, and then at Olmutz, whence the railroad carried me to Vienna, my first stop in that Germany for which I cared only to have done with as quickly as possible, in order to shorten the exile that separated me from home and mother.

Vienna is an animated city. The population there is almost more French than German in its vivacity of character; it has spirit, good-nature, and gayety.

I had no letters of recommendation in Vienna, and knew not a soul there. I took lodgings temporarily at a hotel, with the intention of finding, as soon as possible, a quieter and less expensive location in that city where I was to pass some months, and where it was necessary to regulate my manner of life according to my resources. A traveling companion had advised me to lodge in some private house or family *pension*. An opportunity of putting this advice in practice was soon offered.

Not for anything in the world would I have had my mother make sacrifices for the sake of increasing my little stipend; besides, if I had had the slightest desire for creating useless expense, the example of a life as laborious as hers would have sufficed to take away from me the temptation. My board and lodging, and the cost of admission to the theater, the frequenting of which was necessary to the study of my art, constituted my whole budget, and with care, the amount of my allowance could be made sufficient for all.

The first work that I saw advertised on the billboards of the Vienna Opera was Mozart's *Magic Flute*. I went in haste, and took a ticket for one of the cheapest places, at the top of the house. Unpretentious as was my seat, I would not have exchanged it for an empire.

It was the first time that I had ever heard the admirable score of the *Magic Flute*. I was carried away with delight. The performance was excellent. Otto Nicolaï directed the orchestra. The rôle of the Queen of Night was finely rendered by a singer of much talent, Madame Hasselt-Barth ; that of the High Priest, Sarastro, was sung by an artist of great celebrity,

gifted with an admirable voice, which
he managed with fine method and in
grand style; it was Staudigl. The
other rôles were well sustained, and
I still recall the charming voices of
the trio of boys who filled those of
the Three Genii.

I passed in my card to the director,
stating the fact of my presence there
as a *prix de Rome* student, and re-
questing the privilege of seeing him.
He sent for me, and I was conducted
to him behind the scenes, where he
presented me to the artists, with
whom I found myself, from that time,
in continued relationship. But, as I
did not know a *traitre mot* of German, and the most of the singers
scarcely spoke French any better, it
went rather hard at first.

Fortunately, however, one of the
musicians of the orchestra, to whom
Nicolaï presented me, spoke French.
His name was Lévy, father of Richard
Lévy, then a child of fourteen years,
and who has since held his father's

place at the Vienna Opera. M. Lévy received me most kindly, inviting me to call upon him. In a short time we were the best of friends. There were three other children in the family — the eldest, Carl Lévy, a pianist of great ability, and a distinguished composer; the second, Gustave, to-day a publisher of music in Vienna; and the daughter, Mélanie, a charming person, already married to the harpist, Parish Alwars.

It was to M. Lévy that I owed my acquaintance, after a stay of several weeks, with Count Stockhammer, one of the men most useful to me in Vienna, and who was president of the Philharmonic Society. Lévy, to whom I had shown my mass written in Rome, presented me to the count, and spoke to him of the mass in the most flattering terms. The count offered, with ready kindness, to have it produced at the church of St. Charles, by the soloists, chorus, and orchestra of the Philharmonic

Society. The day chosen was the
14th of September. They seemed
well pleased with my work, of which
fact Count Stockhammer gave me
prompt and substantial proof by asking me to write a requiem mass—
solos, chorus, and orchestra—to be
performed at the same church on the
2d of November, the day of commem-
oration of the dead.

I had only six weeks before me.
It was impossible to be ready at the
date specified without working day
and night, without rest or relaxation.
I accepted the offer with joy, and lost
not an instant. The requiem was
finished at the desired time. One
rehearsal was sufficient to make
everything go admirably, thanks to
the excellence of the general musical
education, nowhere as common as in
Germany, and which it is a pleasure
to observe. I was especially amazed
at the facility with which even
.schoolboys sing at first sight; they
all read music as if it were their

natural tongue. Therefore, the execution of the choruses was perfect. I had, among the soloists, a superb bass singer. It was Draxler, who was then quite young, and divided with Staudigl the place of first bass at the Opera. Since that time, Staudigl has died insane, as I am informed, and Draxler, who replaced him, was still at the theater, twenty-five years later, when I returned to Vienna, for the production of my opera of *Roméo et Juliette.*

Some time before the performance of my requiem, Nicolaï had introduced me to an eminent composer, named Becker, devoted exclusively to chamber music. There was assembled weekly, at his house, a quartette, of which Holz, the first violin, had known Beethoven intimately — a circumstance which, aside from his talent, rendered his presence very interesting. Becker was, besides, perhaps the best accepted musical critic at that time in all

10

Germany. He came to hear my requiem, of which he wrote a very eulogistic report, most encouraging to a young man of my age. He said that this work, "although that of a young artist, still seeking his way and style, revealed a grandeur of conception become very rare at this time."

This great undertaking, accomplished in so few weeks, had worn me out to that extent that I fell ill with severe inflammation of the throat, resulting in an abscess. Not wishing to alarm my mother, I gave reliable and confidential news of my condition only to my friends, the Desgoffes, who were then in Paris. As soon as Desgoffe knew that I was ill in Vienna, he hesitated not an instant; he left his wife and daughter, put aside the pictures he was preparing for the *Salon*, and started off to come and take care of me.

At that time it took nearly five or six days to go from Paris to Vienna.

We were in the dead of winter, in the month of December, and this journey, uncomfortable at any rate in such a season, became still more so by reason of a serious indisposition contracted by my friend on the way. He arrived at Vienna, himself needing to be cared for. He passed not less than twenty-two days at my bedside, sleeping with one eye open, on a mattress spread upon the floor, and watching, with a mother's solicitude, my slightest movement. He did not leave me to return to Paris until the physician assured him of my complete convalescence.

Such friendships are not often met with, and in this respect Providence has especially blessed me.

The success of my requiem resulted in modifying all my plans of sojourn in Germany, by prolonging my residence in Vienna. Count Stockhammer gave me another order, in the name of the Philharmonic Society. It was to write a vocal mass without accompaniment, intended to be executed during Lent, in the same church of St. Charles, my patron saint. I took care not to allow this additional opportunity to escape, first, of trying my powers, and then, of hearing my work — a privilege so rare and valuable at the beginning of a career. This was my second and last undertaking in Vienna, from whence I departed immediately for Berlin, by way of Prague and Dresden, in which latter city I made a short stay for the purpose of seeing the fine museum there, where, among other masterpieces, are found Holbein's celebrated Virgin, and the wonderful Sistine Madonna, due to the brush of Raphael.

Upon my arrival in Berlin I made haste to call upon Madame Henzel, as she had invited me to do; but, in about three weeks, I fell seriously ill again, with inflammation of the bowels, just at the time when I had written to my mother that I was getting ready to leave, and was finally to see her again after a separation of three years and a half.

Madame Henzel sent her physician to see me, to whom I gave the following ultimatum:

"Monsieur, I have a mother in Paris who is waiting for my return, and now counting the intervening hours. If she knows that I am detained from her by illness, she will set out on the journey herself, and might lose her senses on the way. She is advanced in years. I will give her a reason for my detention here, but the delay must be short. Fifteen days is all I can allow you in which to put me under the ground or to set me on my feet."

"Very well," said the doctor, "if you will promise to follow my directions, you can leave in fifteen days."

He kept his word. The fourteenth day I was out of the trouble, and forty-eight hours afterward departed for Leipzig, where Mendelssohn was living, and to whom his sister, Madame Henzel, had given me a letter of introduction.

Mendelssohn received me admirably. I use this word purposely, in order to express the gracious condescension with which a man of such distinction treated a young fellow who could have been nothing more in his opinion than a pupil. During the four days that I passed at Leipzig, I can say that Mendelssohn occupied himself entirely with me. He questioned me concerning my studies and my works, with the liveliest and sincerest interest; he asked to hear, upon the piano, my last composition, and I received from him the most precious words of approbation and encouragement. I will mention but one of them, which I have always been too proud of ever to forget. I had played for him the *Dies Irae* of my Vienna requiem. He placed his hand upon a part of it written for five voices, without accompaniment, and said:

"My friend, this part might be signed by Cherubini."

Words like these, coming from such a great master, are real decorations, and one carries them with more pride than any number of ribbons.

Mendelssohn was director of the *Gewandhaus* Philharmonic Society. This society was not holding its meetings at that time, the concert season having passed; but he had the delicate thoughtfulness to call it together for me, and to let me hear his beautiful work called the *Scotch Symphony, in A minor*, a copy of the score of which he gave me with a word of friendly remembrance from his own hand. Alas! the premature death of this great and charming genius was soon to make of this souvenir a genuine and precious relic! And this death followed six months after that of the lovely sister to whom

I was indebted for the favor of having known her brother.

Mendelssohn did not limit himself to the calling together of the Philharmonic Society. He was an organist of the first order, and wished to acquaint me with several of the numerous and admirable compositions of Sebastian Bach for that instrument, over which he reigned supreme. For this purpose he ordered to be examined and put in good condition the old organ of St. Thomas, formerly played by Bach himself; and there, for more than two hours, he revealed to me wonders of which I had no previous conception; then, to cap the climax of his gracious kindness, he made me a gift of a collection of motets by this same Bach, for whom he had a religious veneration, according to whose school he had been formed from his childhood, and whose grand oratorio of *The Passion According to St. Matthew* he directed and accompanied from memory when only fourteen years old.

Such was the extreme courtesy shown me by that great artist, that eminent musician, who was taken away in the flower of his age — thirty-eight years — from the admiration that he had won, and from the master-works reserved for him by the future. Strange destiny of genius, even the most pleasing! It required the death of him who wrote the exquisite compositions, that are to-day the delight of the subscribers to the concerts of the Conservatory, to win for them favor in the ears that had formerly rejected them.

After having seen Mendelssohn I had but one desire—to return as soon as possible to Paris, and to be again with my poor, dear mother. I set out from Leipzig on the 14th of May, 1843; I changed conveyance seventeen times on the way; of six nights, I passed four in traveling; and, finally, on the 25th of May, I arrived in Paris, where, for me, a new life was to begin. My brother met me upon the arrival of the *diligence*, and together we took our way to that dear home where I was again both to give and find so much joy.

IV.

THE RETURN.

WHETHER it was that three years and a half of absence had so much changed me, or that my last and still recent illness, added to the fatigue of the journey, had so dreadfully altered my looks, my mother did not recognize me at first sight. I had, it is true, an outline of a beard, but so slight was it that I think one might even have counted the rudiments.

During my absence my mother had left the *rue de l'Éperon*, and was living in the *rue Vaneau*, in the parish of the *Missions Étrangères*, the church of which stood at the corner of the *rue de Bac* and the *rue de Babylone*, and in which the new position that I was to occupy for several years awaited me.

The curé of the said parish, Abbé Dumarsais, was formerly my chaplain at the *Lycée St. Louis.* He succeeded Abbé Lecourtier in the vicarage of the *Missions.* During my stay at the Academy of France at Rome, Abbé Dumarsais wrote to me, offering me the position of organist and chapel master of the parish upon my return to Paris. I accepted, but on certain conditions. I did not wish to receive advice, and much less orders, either from the curé, the vestry, or anyone else whomsoever. I had my ideas, my sentiments, my convictions; in short, I wished to be the "curé of music"; otherwise, not at all. This was radical, but my conditions had been accepted; there was no objection to them. Habits are, however, tenacious. The musical *régime* to which my predecessor had accustomed the good parishioners was quite opposite to the tastes and tendencies that I brought back from Rome and Germany. Palestrina and

Bach were my gods, and I was going to burn what the people had until then worshiped.

The resources at my disposal were almost nothing. Besides the organ, which was very mediocre and limited, I had a body of singers composed of two basses, one tenor, a choir-boy, and myself, who filled at the same time the functions of chapel master, organist, singer, and composer. I endeavored to direct the music to the best advantage with this meager force, and the necessity in which I was placed, of making the most of such limited means, proved beneficial to me.

Things went very well at first, but I finally surmised, from a certain coldness and reserve on the part of the parishioners, that I was not entirely in the good graces of my audience. I was not mistaken. Toward the end of the first year my curé called me to him and confessed that he had to suffer complaints and fault-finding from the members of the congregation. Monsieur So-and-So and Madame So-and-So did not find the musical service in the least degree gay or entertaining. The curé then asked me to "modify my style," and to make concessions.

"*Monsieur le Curé*," replied I, "you know our agreement. I am here, not to consult your parishioners; I am here to elevate them. If 'my style' does not please them the case is very plain. I will resign; you may recall my predecessor, and everybody will be satisfied. Take it as it is or leave it alone."

"Very well, then," said the curé, "that is all right; it is understood; I accept your resignation."

And thereupon we separated, the best friends in the world.

I had not been half an hour at home when his servant rang at my door.

"Well, Jean, what is the matter?"

"*Monsieur le Curé* would like to speak with you."

"Ah, very well, Jean; tell him I will be there at once."

Arrived in his presence, he resumed the conversation, saying:

"Come, come, my dear fellow, you threw the helve after the hatchet a while ago. Is there no way of arranging the matter? Let us consider the question calmly. You went off like gunpowder."

"*Monsieur le Curé*, it is useless to begin anew this discussion. I persist in all that I have said. If I must listen to everybody's objections there will be no way of getting along; either I remain entirely independent, or I go. This was our understanding, as you know, and I will abate nothing from it."

"*Ah! mon Dieu*," said he; "what a dreadful man you are!"

Then, after a pause:

"Well, come then, stay."

And from that day he never spoke to me again on this subject, allowing me the most perfect liberty of action.

After that, my most determined oppo-
nents became, little by little, my
warmest supporters, and the small
additions successively made to my
salary indicated the progress made
in the sympathies of my hearers. I
began with twelve hundred francs a
year; this was not much. The second
year they granted me an increase of
three hundred francs, the third year
I had eighteen hundred francs, and
the fourth two thousand. But I must
not anticipate the order of events.

My mother and I lived in the house
with the curé. There was also
living under the same roof an eccle-
siastic three years older than I,
who had been one of my comrades
at the *Lycée St. Louis*—the Abbé
Charles Gay. The differences in
age and class that separated us at the
lyceum would, doubtless, have left us
strangers to each other if a common
interest had not brought us together.
This interest was music. Charles

Gay, who was then fourteen years of age, had great musical aptitude, and sang the part of second soprano in the chapel choir. He was, besides, one of the most brilliant pupils of the school. He finished his studies, and it was nearly three years before we saw each other again. I met him in the foyer of the *Opéra* one night when they were playing *La Juive*. Recognizing him at once, I went directly to him:

"*Comment!*" said he, "it is you. And what has become of you?"

"I am busy with composition."

"Indeed!" replied he, "so am I. And with whom are you studying?"

"With Reicha."

"Well, I declare! and I also. Oh, that is delightful; we must see each other often."

Thus was renewed a friendship begun at school, which has remained one of the cherished affections of my life.

I had great admiration for this

11

friend, in whom I recognized a fine organization and faculties much superior to mine. His compositions seemed to me to reveal a man of genius, and I envied him the future to which it seemed to me he was called. I often went to pass the evening at his house, where there was always a great deal of music. His sister was an excellent pianist, and I there heard (besides his own compositions which were tried before invited friends) the trios of Mozart and Beethoven.

One day I received from this friend, who was then in the country, a line begging me to come and see him, saying that he had something of interest to tell me. I thought that it was a question of marriage. When I arrived where he was stopping, he announced that he was going to be a priest. I then understood the meaning of the folios and other big books with which I had for some time noticed that his table was loaded. I was too young to comprehend the importance of this sudden change of mind, and pitied him for making a choice that would require the sacrifice of a fine future to a fate that seemed to me so unenviable.

Having decided upon this course, he resolved to go and pass some time in Rome, there to begin his theological studies. I had just then carried off the *grand prix*, thus earning the privilege of a two years' stay in Rome, and so it was that I found my friend again in that city, where his arrival preceded mine by three months. On my return from Germany, circumstances brought us still nearer together, by placing us as dwellers under the same roof. To-day a priest of thirty years' standing, vicar-general of his intimate friend, the bishop of Poitiers, the Abbé Gay* has become, by his virtues and his ability as an orator and writer, one

---

* The Abbé Gay has since become, himself, the bishop of Poitiers.

or the most eminent members of the
clergy of France.

Toward the third year of my services as chapel master, I, also, felt a
strong desire to enter ecclesiastical
life. To my musical occupations I
had added philosophical and theological studies, and even attended in
clerical dress, during an entire winter,
the lectures on theology at the semi-
nary of St. Sulpice.

But I was strangely mistaken as to
my own nature and my true vocation.
I realized in time that it would be
impossible for me to live without my
art, and, laying aside the garb for
which I was not adapted, I entered
again into the world. But I owe to
that period of my life a friendship,
the mention of which I consider it an
honor to associate with this history
of my life.

Abbé Dumarsais, Abbé Gay, and I
were sent, during the summer of
1846, to take sea-bathing at Trouville

for our health. One day I came near drowning, and the press made such haste with this incident, that the news was published on the following day in the papers of Paris, whilst my brother, whom, fortunately, I had immediately informed of the danger escaped, was trying, on his part, to reassure my mother by showing her my letter just received. It was announced bluntly that I had been "brought in dead upon a stretcher." Truth has hard work to run as fast as falsehood.

Now, in the course of our bathing season, we met on the shore a most worthy abbé, walking with a young boy whose preceptor he was. This boy of twelve or thirteen years was named Gaston de Beaucourt. His mother, the Countess de Beaucourt, owned a fine estate some leagues from Trouville, near *Pont-l'Évêque la Lisieux*. She invited us in the most courteous and gracious manner to visit there before returning to Paris.

This dear, lovely boy, to-day a man of forty-three years of age, and one of the best of men, became a life-long friend. I owe to his affection, so sure, so firm and tender, not only the joys afforded by such a perfect friendship, but also proofs of the most complete and steadfast devotion.

The revolution of February, 1848, had just broken out when I left the musical leadership of the *Missions Etrangères*. I had filled a position for four years and a half, which, while very useful and profitable in the way of musical studies, had, nevertheless, the disadvantage of leaving me to vegetate, as far as my career and future were concerned, in a position without prospect of advancement. For a composer, there is hardly but one road to follow in order to make a name, and that is the theater.

The theater is the place where one

finds the opportunity and the way to speak every day to the public; it is a daily and permanent exposition opened to the musician.

Religious music and the symphony are certainly of a higher order, abstractly considered, than dramatic music, but the opportunities and the means of making one's self known along those lines are rare, and appeal only to an intermittent public, rather than to a regular public, like that of the theater. And then what an infinite variety for a dramatic author in the choice of subjects! What a field opened to the fancy, to imagination, and to romance! The theater tempted me. I was then nearly thirty years of age, and was impatient to try my powers upon this new field of battle. But I had need of a poem, and knew no author from whom I could obtain one. I needed, also, to find a director interested in me, and who would consent to entrust me with the composition of an opera.

Who was likely to be so disposed, considering the religious character of my antecedents, and my inexperience in the theater? No one. I saw myself in an inextricable difficulty.

But circumstances placed in my path a man who shed upon me a light. This was the violinist, Seghers, director at that time of the concerts of the St. Cecilia Society, in the *rue Chaussée-d-Antin*. The opportunity was given me at these concerts for the hearing of a number of pieces that produced a good impression. Seghers knew the Viardot family. Madame Viardot was then in all the glory of her talent and fame. It was in 1849, at the time when she first created, in so masterly a manner, the rôle of *Fidès* in Meyerbeer's *Prophète*. Madame Viardot received me with the best of grace, inviting me to bring some of my compositions for her to hear. I made haste to accept this offer, and passed several hours with her at the piano. After having listened to me with the kindest interest, she said :

" But, Monsieur Gounod, why do you not write an opera?"

"Eh! Madame," replied I, "I could ask nothing better, but I have no poem."

"What! You know no one who could write you one?"

"Some one who could, *mon Dieu*, perhaps; but who would—that is another thing. I know, or rather, I did know in my childhood, Émile Augier, with whom I played at rolling hoop in the Luxembourg gardens; but Augier has since become famous. I have no celebrity, and the playfellow of childhood would hardly care to play over again a game otherwise hazardous than a turn at hoops."

"Well," said Madame Viardot, "go and see Augier, and tell him that I will sing the principal rôle in your opera, if he will write the poem."

One may guess if I waited to be told the second time! I ran to Augier, who received my proposition with open arms.

" Madame Viardot !" cried he; "yes, to be sure ! and that immediately !"

Nestor Roqueplan was then director of the *Opéra*. Upon the recommendation of Madame Viardot, he consented to allow a part of the time of performance, but not the whole evening. It was necessary, then, to find a subject uniting three essential conditions—first, to be short ; second, to be serious ; and third, to have a female rôle as the principal figure. We decided upon *Sapho*. The study of the opera could not be undertaken until the following year, and, furthermore, Augier had to first finish a grand subject upon which he was occupied at that time. It was, I believe, *Diana*, for Mademoiselle Rachel.

Finally, I had his promise to begin, and waited with mingled impatience and tranquility.

A sad event came to afflict our family at the moment when I was about setting myself to work. It was in the month of April, 1850. Augier had just finished the poem of *Sapho*, when, on the 2d of April, my brother fell ill. On the 3d, I signed with Roqueplan the contract, according to which I engaged to deliver to him the score of *Sapho* on the 30th of September, at the latest. I had six months in which to compose and write an opera in three acts — my *début* at the theater. On the night of the 6th of April my brother passed away. It was a dreadful blow to my mother and to all of us.

He left a widow, the mother of a child of two years, and of another little being coming into the world seven months later, in the midst of tears; and whose destiny it was to be born on the 2d of November, the very day when the church mourns with her children for those whom they have lost. This situation of affairs brought about difficulties and complications in life of which it was necessary to think immediately. The question of guardianship of the children; of succession in my brother's business as an architect, in which his death left a host of affairs unfinished; all the consequences, finally, of so sudden and unforeseen a calamity demanded for a month my personal attention to the regulation of the interests, and the arrangements for living, of my poor, prostrated, and inconsolable sister-in-law. Furthermore, my unhappy mother seemed almost to lose her reason under the stunning blow by which she had been smitten. Everything in and around me conspired to render me incapable of devoting myself to the work for which I had already so little time.

At the end of a month, however, I began to think of occupying myself again with the composition so urgently demanding my attention. Madame Viardot, who was then singing in Germany, and whom I had advised of the misfortune with which we had been visited, wrote me at once, suggesting that I go with my mother to a place owned by her in Brie, where I could find, as she said, the solitude and quiet of which I had need.

I followed her advice, and my mother and I left Paris to go and stay for a while in the house where the mother of Madame Viardot (Madame Garcia, widow of the celebrated singer) was living, in company with a sister of Monsieur Viardot and a young daughter (the oldest of the children), to-day Madame Héritte — a remarkable musical composer. I also met there a charming man, Ivan Tourguéneff, the eminent Russian writer, a most excellent man, and an intimate friend of the Viardot family. I set myself to work immediately upon my arrival. Strange fact! It seems as if sad and pathetic accents should have been the first to thrill the fibers of my being, so recently shaken by the most painful emotions! But it was to the contrary; the brigther

scenes were those that first seized
and took possession of me, as if my
nature, bent under the weight of sorrow and mourning, felt the need of
reaction and of free respiration after
those hours of agony and days of
tears and sighs.

Thanks to the calm which reigned
around me, my work advanced more
rapidly than I had expected. Madame
Viardot, after her season in Germany,
was called by her engagements to
England. Returning from that
country at the beginning of September, she found my opera nearly finished. I hastened to let her hear the
composition, for her impressions of
which I waited with the greatest
anxiety. She expressed herself
pleased with it, and in a few days
she was so well acquainted with the
score that she accompanied herself
upon the piano almost entirely from
memory. That was, perhaps, the
most extraordinary feat of musical
memorizing of which I was ever wit-

ness, and one which shows the aston-
ishing ability of that wonderful artist.

Sapho was represented at the *Opéra*
for the first time on the 16th of April,
1851. I was then nearly thirty-two
years old. It was not a success, and
yet this *début* gave me a good place
in the estimation of artists. While
the work showed inexperience in
what is called stage business, a lack of
knowledge of dramatic effects, of resources, and of practice in instrumentation, there was, at the same
time, a true feeling in expression, an
instinct generally correct on the lyric
side of the subject, and a tendency to
nobility of style. The close of the
first act produced an impression completely surprising. It was called for
again, with unanimous applause, in
which I could hardly believe, although
my ears were ringing with unex-
pected emotion, and this "*bis*" was
repeated at each of the following
representations. The effect of the
second act was inferior to that of the

first, notwithstanding the success of a *cantilena* sung by Madame Viardot, and that of the airy duo between Brémond and Mademoiselle Poinsot, "*Va m'attendre, mon maître.*" But the third act was very well received. A rehearing was demanded of the shepherd's song, "*Broutez le thym, broutez mes chèvres;*" and the final lines of *Sapho*, "*O ma lyre immortelle,*" were highly applauded.

The shepherd's song was the *début* of the tenor, Aymès; he sang it marvelously well, thereby making his reputation. Gueymard and Marié filled the rôles of *Phaon* and of *Alcée.*

My mother was naturally present at the first representation. As I was leaving the stage to rejoin her in the hall, where she was waiting for me after the exit of the public, I met Berlioz in the lobby of the *Opéra*, his eyes filled with tears. I sprang to his neck, saying:

"Oh! my dear Berlioz, come show those eyes to my mother! that would be the best criticism she could read upon my work."

Berlioz yielded to my wishes, and approaching my mother, said:

"Madame, I do not remember to have felt a similar emotion in twenty years."

He published an account of *Sapho*, which is, assuredly, one of the highest and most flattering tributes that I have had the honor and good fortune to gather in my career.

This opera was played only six times. The engagement of Madame Viardot came to a close, and she was replaced in the rôle by Mademoiselle Masson, with whom it had only three more representations.

It may be set down as a principle, I think, that a dramatic work always has, or nearly so, all the success that it deserves with the public. Theatrical success is the result of such a combination of elements that it suffices (examples of which are abundant) for the absence of any one of

12

these elements, sometimes of the most accessory, to counteract and compromise the effect of the highest qualities. The stage-setting, the ballet, the scenery, the costumes, the libretto — so many things contribute to the success of an opera! The attention of the public needs to be sustained and satisfied with the variety of the spectacle. There are works of the first order in certain respects that have gone under, not in the admiration of artists, but in the public favor, from the lack of the condiment necessary to secure their acceptance by those for whom the simple attraction of the beautiful does not suffice.

I do not pretend, by any means, to demand for the fate of *Sapho* the benefit of these considerations. The public brings to the formation of opinion upon any work certain rights and titles constituting a kind of province and authority apart. One can not expect or demand of it the special

knowledge by which the technical
value of a work of art is decided;
but it has on its side the right to
expect and demand that a dramatic
work should respond to the instincts
for which it seeks nourishment and
gratification at the theater. Now, a
dramatic composition does not depend exclusively upon the qualities
of form and style; these qualities are
certainly essential; they are even
indispensable in preserving a work
from the rapid attacks of Time,
whose scythe restrains itself only in
the presence of ideal beauty; but
they are neither the only qualities,
nor even, in a certain sense, the first;
they consolidate and strengthen dramatic success—they do not establish
it.

The public of the theater is a *dy-
namometer*. It seeks not to know the
value of a work from the point of
view of taste; it measures only the
power of the passion and the degree
of the emotions excited; that is to say,

what makes of it really a dramatic
work, an expression of what goes on
in the human soul, individual or col-
lective. From which it results that
author and public are reciprocally
called to instruct each other in mat-
ters of art—the public instructing the
author by showing its discernment
and approval of the true, and the
author teaching the public by initia-
ting it into the elements and conditions of the beautiful. Outside of
this view of the question, it seems to
me impossible to explain the strange
phenomenon of the incessant change-
ability of the public, rejecting in the
morning what moved it to passion
the night before, and crucifying to-
day what it will worship to-morrow.

Although *Sapho* was not fated to
be what is called a popular success, it
was not without results advantageous
to my musical career and to my
future. In the first place, Ponsard
asked me on the very evening of the

first representation, to write the music for the choruses in *Ulysse*, a tragedy in five acts, intended by him for the *Théâtre Français*. I accepted the offer upon the spot, without knowing the work; but the reputation of the author of *Lucrèce*, of *Charlotte Corday*, and of *Agnès de Méranie* was a sufficient guarantee of the importance of the work, to the collaboration of which I had the good fortune to be called.

Arsène Houssaye was then the director of the *Comédie-Française*. It was necessary to add to the usual *personnel* of the theater a chorus troop and a reinforcement of the regular orchestra.*

Ulysse was produced the 18th of June, 1852. I had just married, a few days before, a daughter of Zimmerman,† the celebrated professor of the piano at the Conserv-

---

* See in appendix, letter from Berlioz to Gounod, dated November 19, 1851.

† See in appendix, letter from Gounod to Lefuel, without date.

atory, and to whom is due the fine school from which have come Prudent, Marmontel, Goria, Lefébure-Wély, Ravina, Bizet, and many others. I became, by this alliance, brother-in-law of the young painter, Édouard Dubufe, who was already most ably carrying his father's name, the heritage and reputation of which his own son, Guillaume Dubufe, promises to brilliantly maintain.

The principal rôles of *Ulysse* were taken by Mademoiselle Judith, Messieurs Geffroy, Delaunay, Maubant, Mademoiselle Nathalie, and others. The musical part included not less than fourteen choruses, a tenor solo, several passages of instrumental melodrama, and an orchestral introduction. There was, for the composer, a certain danger of monotony in the constant employment of the same resources — the orchestra and the choruses.

I had the good fortune, nevertheless, to get very happily around the difficulty, and this second work earned me another good point in the opinion of artists. My score had, besides, a great advantage not possessed by that of *Sapho*, for which no publisher presented himself. Messieurs Escudier did me the honor to engrave my new work without charge.

Ulysse was played forty times. It was the second trial in my dramatic career of which my mother was witness.

The choruses of *Ulysse* seem to me to be conceived in correct character and color, and in individual style. The management of the orchestra leaves something to be desired with respect to experience, rather than to that of coloring, the instinct of which is, in general, very happy.

A few days after my marriage, I was appointed director of the *Orphéon*, and of vocal instruction in the public schools of Paris. In this position I replaced M. Hubert, pupil and successor to Wilhem, founder of that branch of instruction.

These functions, filled during eight years and a half, exercised a most happy influence over my musical career, by the experience they afforded me in the direction and handling of large vocal forces, treated in a style simple and favorable to their best sonority.

My third musical attempt for the theater was *La Nonne Sanglante,* an opera in five acts, with text by Scribe and Germain Delavigne. Nestor Roqueplan, who was still director of the *Opéra,* had a great admiration for *Sapho,* and sincere friendship for me. He used to say that he found in me a tendency " to do things on a grand scale." It was he who wished me to write for the *Opéra* a work in five acts. *La Nonne Sanglante* was written in 1852-1853. Put in rehearsal October 18, 1853; laid aside

and afterward taken up several
times for study, it finally came to
the footlights on October 18, 1854,
exactly a year after it was first begun.
It had only eleven representations,
after which Roqueplan was replaced
in the direction of the *Opéra* by M.
Crosnier. The new director having
declared that he would not allow
"such filth" to be played any longer,
the piece disappeared from the billboards, and has never been seen
there since.

This caused me some regret. The
satisfactory amount of the receipts
certainly did not warrant so radical
and summary a measure. But manâ-
gerial decisions sometimes have, it is
said, an under side that it is useless to
think of penetrating. In such a case,
pretexts are given; the real reasons
remain concealed. I do not know if
La Nonne Sanglante was susceptible
of enduring success, but I do not
think so. Not that it was a work
without effect (it contained several

striking scenes), but the subject was
too uniformly somber. It had,
besides, the disadvantage of being
more than imaginary, more than im-
probable ; it was beyond the limits
of the possible, resting upon a purely
fanciful foundation, without reality,
and, consequently, without dramatic
interest, there being no interest outside of the true, or, at least, the probable.

I think that my part of this work
showed substantial progress in the
employment of the orchestra. Certain pages therein are treated with a
surer knowledge of instrumentation,
and with a more experienced hand.
Several parts are well colored ; among
others, the song of the *Crusade* by
Peter the Hermit and chorus, in the
first act ; in the second act, the sym-
phonic prelude of the *Ruins*, and the
march of the *Ghosts;* in the third act,
a *cavatina* by the tenor, and his duo
with the *Nonne*.

My principal interpreters were

Mesdemoiselles Wertheimber and
Poinsot, Messieurs Gueymard, De-
passio, and Merly.

I consoled myself for my mortifi-
cation by writing a symphony (No. 1,
in D) for the Society of Young
Artists, just founded by Pasdeloup,
and whose concerts took place in the
Salle Herz, rue de la Victoire. This
symphony was well received, and I
was thus encouraged to write another
for the same society (No. 2, in E flat),
which also met with a certain success. I also wrote, at this epoch, the
Messe Solennelle de Sainte Cécile, which
was brought out successfully for the
first time by the *Association des
Artistes Musiciens,* on the 22d of
November, 1855, at the church of St.
Eustache, and which has been performed several times since. It is
dedicated to the memory of my
father-in-law, Zimmerman, whom we
lost on October 29, 1853.

Still another misfortune fell upon

our family. On the 6th of August,
1855, death took from us an elder
sister of my wife, Juliette Dubufe
(wife of Édouard Dubufe, the painter),
a woman gifted with a rare combination of the most charming qualities,
added to exceptional talent as a
sculptor and pianist. *"Bonté, esprit,
talent"*—such was the simple inscrip-
tion, as well merited as eloquent, that
summed up the praise and the regrets
inspired by this woman whose exquisite grace irresistibly captivated all
who approached her.

The leadership of the *Orphéon*
then occupied the greater part of
my time. I wrote for the large
choral reunions of the organization
a number of compositions, of which
some were especially remarked ; and
among these are two masses, one of
which was performed under my direction, June 12, 1853, in the church of
St. Germain-l' Auxerrois, in Paris. It
was during the time of one of the

grand annual meetings of the *Orphéon*, June 8, 1856, that my wife presented me with a son. (Three years before, on the 13th of the same month, we had the sorrow of losing at birth our first-born child, a girl.) On the morning of the day when my son was born, my brave wife, although feeling the first pains of motherhood just as I was starting out for the meeting of the *Orphéon*, had the force to conceal from me her sufferings, and when in the afternoon I returned to the house my son was already in the world.

The coming of this child, so much desired, was an occasion of joy and feasting. We have been so fortunate as to bring him up; he has now passed his twenty-first year, and is destined to be a painter.

After *La Nonne Sanglante*, I did not work at any other dramatic composition, but wrote a small oratorio, *Tobie*, at the request of George Hainl, then orchestra director at the *Grand Théâtre* at Lyons, for one of his annual benefit concerts. This work had, I think, some qualities of senti- ment and of expression. Especial notice was taken of a very touching air in the part of the young *Tobie*, and of some other passages not lack- ing in a certain pathetic effect.

In 1856, I made the acquaintance of Jules Barbier and of Michel Carré. I asked them if they were disposed to work with me, and to entrust to me a poem, to which they consented with great willingness. The first subject to which I called their atten- tion was *Faust*. This idea impressed them favorably. We went to see M. Carvalho, at that time director of the *Théâtre-Lyrique*, in the *Boulevard du Temple*, where they had just mounted *La Reine Topaze*, by Victor Massé, and in which Madame Miolan-Carvalho had achieved a brilliant success. Our project pleased M. Carvalho, and my collaborators set themselves im-

mediately to work. I had finished
nearly half of my part when M. Carvalho informed me that the theater
of *La Porte-Saint-Martin* had in prep-
aration a grand melodrama entitled
Faust, which circumstance overturned
all his calculations in regard to our
work. He was of the opinion, and
with good reason, that it would be
impossible for us to be ready before the *Porte-Saint-Martin*, and, furthermore, he considered it unwise,
from the point of view of financial
success, to engage in a contest upon
the same subject with a theater,
the luxury of whose stage-mounting
would already have attracted all Paris
before our opera could be produced.

He advised us, then, to choose
another subject, but this discomfiture
had rendered me incapable of apply-
ing my mind to anything else, and I
remained eight days without the force
to undertake other work.

Finally, M. Carvalho requested me
to write a comedy, and to seek my

inspiration at the theater of Molière. This was the beginning of *Le Méd-ecin Malgré Lui*, produced at the *Théâtre-Lyrique* on the 15th of January, 1858, the anniversary of the birth of Molière. The announcement of a comedy written by a musician whose first efforts seemed to indicate quite different tendencies, caused a presentiment and fear of failure. The result set at naught these fears, some of which were, perhaps, not without hope, and *Le Médecin Malgré Lui* was, *malgré cela*, my first popular success at the theater. This pleasure was empoisoned by the death of my dear mother, who, after an illness of two months, and having been totally blind for two years, expired on the very next·day after the first representation, January 16, 1858, at the age of seventy-seven and a half years. It was not given to me to bring to her last days the consolation of this fruit and reward of a life wholly consecrated to the interests of her sons. I trust, at least, that she carried with her the hope and premonition that her efforts had not been in vain, and that her sacrifices were blessed.

Le Médecin Malgré Lui enjoyed an uninterrupted series of one hundred representations. It was mounted with great care, and the actor, M. Got, of the *Comédie-Française*, had, by request of our director, the kindness to personally give the assistance of his valuable advice to the artists, in the traditional setting of the piece and the declamation of the spoken dialogue. The principal rôle, that of Sganarelle, was created by Meillet, a rotund and spirited baritone, who obtained in this part a great success, both as a singer and an actor. The other male rôles were entrusted to Girardot, Wartel, Fromant, and Lesage (afterward replaced by Potel and Gabriel), who acquitted themselves well. The two principal female rôles were taken by Mesdemoiselles

13

Faivre and Girard, both full of spirit and gayety. This score, the first that I had occasion to write in a comic vein, is in light and easy style, somewhat similar to Italian opera-bouffe. In certain passages I tried to recall the style of Lully, but the work, as a whole, is in modern form and partakes of the French school. Among the parts most enjoyed were the *Chanson des Glougous*, capitally sung by Meillet, and always called for the second time; the *Trio de la Bastonnade*, the *Sextuor de la Consultation*, a *Fabliau*, the *Scène de Consultation des Paysans*, and a duo between Sganarelle and the nurse.

The *Faust* of the *Porte Saint-Martin* came to a representation, but not even the elegance of the mounting could assure to this melodrama a very long run. M. Carvalho then took up again our first project, and I busied myself at once in finishing the work interrupted to write *Le Médecin Malgré Lui*.

Faust was put in rehearsal in the

month of September, 1858. I gave a hearing of it to M. Carvalho, in the green-room of the theater, on July 1st, before my departure for Switzerland, where I was going to spend the vacation, with my wife and boy, then two years old. At this time, nothing was decided upon as to the distribution of the rôles, and M. Carvalho requested me to allow Madame Carvalho, who lived opposite the theater, to be present at the hearing given him. She was so deeply impressed with the part of Marguerite that M. Carvalho begged me to assign that rôle to her. This was agreed upon, and the future proved this choice to be a veritable inspiration.

But the rehearsals for *Faust* were not destined to be pursued without meeting difficulties. The tenor to whom the title rôle had been assigned, could not, although possessing a charming voice and attractive physique, sustain the weight of this heavy and important part. Some days before the time fixed for the first representation, we were obliged to think of replacing him, and had recourse to Barbot, who was then available. In one month Barbot learned the rôle and was ready to play, and the opera was brought out for the first time on the 19th of March, 1859.

The first production of *Faust* did not create a remarkable impression; it is, however, at this time, my greatest theatrical success. Can it be said to be my best work? Positively I do not know. At any rate, I see in it a confirmation of the thought expressed above, upon the subject of success, namely, that success is rather the result of a certain combination of fortuitous circumstances and favorable conditions, than a proof or measure of the intrinsic value of the work itself. It is by the surface that the favor of the public is first gained; it is by the depth that it is maintained and strengthened. It requires a certain length of time to seize and take to one's self the expression and the meaning of the infinite number of details of which a drama is composed.

The dramatic art is a kind of portrait painting. It should interpret characters as a painter reproduces a face or an attitude; it should gather up and fix all the features, all the inflections, so variable and fleeting, which, taken together, form the individuality of physiognomy that is called a personage. Such are the immortal characters of Hamlet, of Richard III., of Othello, and of Lady Macbeth, in Shakspeare; impersonations having such a resemblance to the type of which they are the expression, that they remain in the memory like a living reality; therefore, they are justly called creations. Dramatic music is subject to this same law, outside of which it has no existence; its object is to specialize physiognomies. Now, that which painting represents simultaneously to the mind, music can only say successively; this is why it escapes so easily from first impressions.

None of my works written before *Faust* gave any reason to expect a score of this kind; nothing had prepared the public for it. It was then, in this respect, a surprise, as it was also with regard to the interpretation. Certainly Madame Carvalho had not been waiting for the rôle of Marguerite to reveal the masterly qualities of execution and style which place her in the front rank of the singers of our day; but no other rôle had afforded her, until that time, the opportunity of showing, to this same degree, the superior phases of her talent, so sure, so refined, so steady and tranquil — I mean its lyric and pathetic qualities. The rôle of Marguerite established her reputation in this respect, and she has left upon this character an imprint which will remain one of the glories of her brilliant career. Barbot showed himself a great musician in the difficult rôle of *Faust*. Balanqué, who created the part of Mephistopheles, was an intelligent comedian whose play, physique, and voice lent themselves wonderfully to this fantastic and Satanic personage. In spite of a little exaggeration in gesture and irony, he succeeded well. The small rôle of Siebel, and that of Valentin, were very acceptably taken by Mademoiselle Faivre and M. Raynal.

As to the score, it was so much discussed that I had no great hope of success

APPENDIX.

I.

To MONSIEUR H. LEFUEL, *Architect*,
At the Academy of France,
Villa Medici, Rome.

NAPLES, Tuesday, July 14, 1840.

I should have been pleased, my dear Hector, to address to you earlier these few lines that I now remit by Murat,* but I have not even yet found time to write to my brother a sufficiently long *pancarte*, for having formed some acquaintances in this city of Naples, three months ago, I had to begin this time by making myself known. And now, from to-day, I shall be more at liberty.

I have also written to Desgoffe, and I should like to have done as much for our good Hébert, to whom I beg you

---

* Murat (Jean), painter, *prix de Rome*.

to make many excuses for me. He shall certainly have news from me directly, one of these days, and that soon, probably, for I expect (although I am not quite sure) to leave on Wednesday or Thursday of the coming week, to make my trip to the islands of Ischia and Capri, returning by Pæstum, Salerna, Amalfi, Sorrento, Pompeii, and Naples. It will be an affair of twelve days.

I hope, my dear, good friend, that you have been well since my departure. I have inquired of Desgoffe regarding you, whom I begged to persuade you not to work too hard. The heat there must be great at this time. Here in Naples it is sometimes very oppressive; to-day, especially, we have had over-powering, sultry weather, but the sea-breeze is invigorating, and we who are lodged almost upon the sea enjoy and take in as much of its freshness as possible.

Naples wearies me more than ever (the city, you understand). I am very curious to see Capri and Ischia, also Pæstum. I went up finally, yesterday,

to Camaldoli; it is an admirable point
of view, especially for expanse of sea.
You know how well we love the sea!
The more one gazes at it, the better
one appreciates the beauty of that
simple, horizontal line, beyond which
may be imagined the infinite.

To-morrow afternoon, at four o'clock,
should it be fine, we are to go up
Vesuvius to see the sunset, and shall
pass the night there in order to get the
effect of the whole bay by moonlight;
and the following morning we shall
see the sunrise. You perceive that
that is a fine plan.

I received, day before yesterday, a
letter from my mother, sent from Rome.
I thank you, dear Hector, if it is to you
that I owe the arrival of this letter. My
mother sends you a thousand compliments, as does also my good Urbain.

How did you like M. Ingres' picture?
Write me your opinion, or send a word
in Desgoffe's letter when he answers
me. Always forward your letters to
the "Ville de Rome, Quai St. Lucie,
Naples." If I should happen to be

out on an excursion in the meanwhile, they will be there upon my
return. Tell Hébert that I should
be very glad to know the effect produced upon his mind by M. Ingres'
picture. Although I do not deserve to
have news from him before writing
myself, I desire this greatly.

Kind regards to my little brother,
Vauthier, whom I beg, also, not to forget me. Tell Fleury* that I regretted
not being able to say good-by to him
before my departure. Finally, I charge
you, my dear friend, with all my
remembrances for our good comrades,
in general and in particular, according
to the recognized formula.

Adieu, dear Hector; I embrace you
as I love you, which is, as you well
know, with all my heart.

CHARLES GOUNOD.

Guénepin† will write you in a few

---

* Confidential servant of the students, having
been then for forty years in the service of the
Academy.

† Guénepin (François-Jean-Baptiste), architect, *prix de Rome.*

days, and will tell you a thousand
pleasant things. He is very good to me
and we have had a pleasant journey,
although our nights have been but three
or four hours long, at the most ; this is,
however, only a detail.

Be so kind as to tell me, when you
write, if Desgoffe has sent to Prince
Soutzo's house for my score of *Der
Freischütz.*

II.

To Monsieur H. Lefuel,
      Venice, Poste Restante.

Rome, Tuesday, April 4, 1841.
My Dear and Loving Father:[*]
Here is your desolated child, racking
his brains to know where to write to
you, and commencing to despair of the
affection of his old papa, when he
learned through M. Schnetz, that that
intrepid centenarian had taken himself
from Florence to Bologna, in order to
reach Venice in the quickest way. It

----

[*] See page 70.

is there, then, in Venice that this son, being reassured, hastens to address his father to say that he is well, and finally, that his mass has met with great success ; in the first place, among his little comrades, and in the second, with the public. He has thought, also, of the gratification this fact would afford his old father, which thought has counted for much in the joy of his success.

This son has also much regretted the absence of this same old father, who is naturally the one to whom he is most attached, and from whom separation at this time is most inopportune for him.

Furthermore, I have letters from Paris charging me with a thousand kind regards for you, my dear, good Hector. I do not know how it happened, but mamma seemed to think that I was going to see you again in two or three months. I have set her mind right upon this point, but the disillusion must have cost her some pain.

And now then, you do not know the news that I have received regarding Urbain. At first it gave me a tremen-

dous spring of joy, but at the end of the
paragraph there came a fearful reaction.
In short, it seems there was some talk
of his making a trip to Sicily and Rome,
but it has fallen through, and I will tell
you how it all happened.

M. le Marquis de Crillon, who has
always felt great interest in our family,
intended to take with him for a traveling companion in Sicily, some good
artist of thorough attainments — an
earnest, serious man — in short, he had
thought of Urbain. He came to our .
house one day and made this proposition to my mother. She thanked him
for his extreme kindness, expressed her
gratitude, and spoke to Urbain of the
plan when she saw him. He, having
quickly and thoroughly decided to
accept the offer, gave an affirmative
reply to M. Crillon. But when it finally
came to the point of going to bid farewell to his patrons, he everywhere met
faces sad and dejected at seeing him go
away, and everywhere expressions of
regret; no one could be found to replace
him in tact, judgment, honesty, etc.—

in short, in all the good and estimable qualities which you know him to possess. This was already a circumstance to hinder the plan of his departure, but it was not all. Something else came to clog the wheels, and this was a business affair in which he found his interests involved to the extent of ten or twelve thousand francs. His presence in Paris became indispensable at this time, as you can readily understand. I am very uneasy regarding the outcome of this critical affair, and should like to know as soon as possible how it has turned. I will inform you about it in my next letter. Poor Urbain ! he is so good, and has given himself so much trouble! Fortunately, he has great courage, and knows how to sustain vexatious trials, but it is hard for the moment.

I found out, dear Hector, that you had written to Gruyère; but at the moment when I was giving way to my jealousy, Hébert said to me: "Console yourself; it was only a commission with which he charged him." Then I comforted myself in the hope of hearing from you later.

I must tell you that I have been very much pleased with the evidences of interest shown in me lately by several of our comrades — among others, our good little painter, Hébert. I appreciated most highly the careful attention with which I noticed him listening to the rehearsal of my mass. This, certainly, would not have been the case had he been indifferent, and one is always glad to mention those who are not so. As I know that you, also, love Hébert, I am glad to give you this information concerning him, being sure that his attachment for me will in nowise diminish yours for him. He is, also, quite well, and sends you a thousand compliments, as do, also, all the other young men at the Academy. I am going to see if he is in his room, and will tempt him to add two words at the end of my letter.

Bazin has not yet arrived. I do not know what he is doing. I am afraid that his native city, in the enthusiasm it must have shown him while passing through, may have taken him bodily and set him upon a pedestal as a statue in his own honor. The Marseillaise are hot-headed; they are capable of having done so with him; that would be a good joke for his prospects as a student here.

Adieu, my dear Hector; you know how well I love you. *Eh, bien,* I embrace you "upon the two cheeks and the left eye," as they say. If you are still with Courtépée,* tell him that I send him, also, a warm grasp of the hand.

I hope that you are both well. If you are having the same weather as with us you ought to do some fine things. Adieu, dear friend.

Yours, with all my heart,
CHARLES GOUNOD.

MY DEAR ARCHITECT:
I profit by the opportunity offered by our dear musician to give you a sign of life. I have learned through our great sculptor, Gruyère, that you have had a succession of colds, and I hope that the sunshine of the noble and

---

*Architect, assistant to Lefuel.

voluptuous Venice will melt the ice that old winter has heaped up in your brain.

You have had a great success at the Exposition; all were astonished at your drawings — the ambassador and ambassadress could not sleep for thinking of them.

I say nothing of myself; what I have done is of too little importance, and not good enough to merit a line. The mass of our celebrated musician met with great success amongst us, and with the public. It was well performed—thanks to the activity he displayed in shaking up the old sleepy-heads.

If you see Loubens* tell him many things for me; and Courtépée, what have you done with him? Have you succeeded in making him get up when you do, oh, early morning worker?

Adieu. If I can be useful or agreeable to you, I am at your service.

E. Hébert.

---

* Former pupil of the Polytechnic School, friend of Gounod, Hébert, etc.

Murat does not want to add two
words; he says he will write you soon.

CHARLES GOUNOD.

That is not true.

MURAT.

III.

To MONSIEUR H. LEFUEL,
    Genoa, Poste Restante.

If M. Lefuel does not come to claim
his letters at Genoa, please forward
this to him at the Academy of France,
at Rome.

VIENNA, Monday,
    August 21, 1842.

MY DEAR HECTOR:

I received, the other week, a letter
from Hébert, whom I was the first to
write to from Vienna. He informs me
that you are somewhere around Genoa,
but can not tell me exactly where. As
you have neglected me all along my
journey, and I have not found, either at
Florence, or Venice, or Vienna, a line

from you, I find myself obliged to ask of some mutual friend if, by accident, he happens to know your address and can give it to me. By the reply I received from Hébert, I saw that he had been more fortunate than I, since he knew, at least, where you were, and where he could give you news of himself while receiving the same from you. You know, however, very well, abominable and unnatural father, how happy would have been your son in seeing a few lines from you; but the whole length of the journey, and not even the first stroke of an "A"! And I, on my part, how could I write to you? I wished to do so everywhere, but nowhere did you give me the means to do so. Even now, I fear that this letter will find you flown away from where you were, so that this uncertainty has decided me to take the precaution that you will observe in the address of this letter. If I were near you, wouldn't I scold you right hard! How is it? Have your patriarchal affections, then, degenerated to the

point of having no further need of
sending a few of those kind lines of
which you know your first-born son
is so appreciative? With merely your
name and address, if you had not the
time to write, I could, at least, have
kept you informed of all that has
concerned me, and still concerns me to-
day — things to which I can not believe
you indifferent. Finally, dear and well
beloved father and friend, now that
I have scolded you, I will forget all
your iniquities; I pardon you from the
bottom of my heart; I have known for
a long time that you dislike to write; I
know, also, that you do not waste your
time, of which I had the proof too often
in Rome, to lay to the score of laziness
the lack of news from you. So, then,
all is forgotten, except yourself.

I should have been glad to tell you,
a long time ago, the good fortune that
has happened to me here — that is the
opportunity of having performed with
grand orchestra, on the 8th of September, in one of the churches of Vienna,
my mass written in Rome, and played

there at *St. Louis-des-Français*, at the king's fête. It is a great privilege, and one which has never before been accorded to any student. I owe it to the acquaintance of some very kind artists who have presented me to people of influence. In Vienna, I work; I see but very few people. I hardly ever go out; I am up to the neck in a requiem with grand orchestra, which will probably be performed in Germany on the 2d of November. An offer has already been made me for the performance of my requiem in the church where my mass will be played, but as I do not know how well I shall be satisfied with the execution of the latter, I have not yet decided with regard to the requiem.

Through the acquaintanceship of Madame Henzel and of Mendelssohn, it is quite possible that I might obtain, in Berlin, a much finer performance than in Vienna, which would have the advantage of placing me in a better position in the opinion of artists. I am still free to accept the offer in this city. If I am satisfied with the execution of my mass on the 8th of September, I shall decide to give my requiem here; if not, I shall take it to Berlin. Madame Henzel, when in Rome, said to me: "When you come to Germany, if you have music to be played, my brother can be of great assistance to you." I wrote to her in Berlin a few days ago, and, as I am to leave here on the 12th of September to make a journey to Munich, Leipzig, Berlin, Dresden, and Prague, I have begged her to inform me if she thinks whether or not I can go to Berlin with prospects of having my music played there. Her reply will influence my decision in this respect. If she replies affirmatively, I shall remain in Berlin until the first days of November, and then return directly to Paris; if not, I shall be obliged to return to Vienna, which I can reach in three or four days by railway. There is one which goes from Vienna to Olmutz, nearly sixty leagues in length. If I am to remain in Berlin for my requiem, I shall be obliged to arrange my journey differently, in this way: Munich, Prague,

Dresden, Leipzig, Berlin. At any rate, I will inform you when I am certain with regard to it.

I have many times regretted our beautiful Rome, dear Hector, and I envy the fate of those who are still there. It is almost entirely in the remembrance of that beautiful country that I now find any delight or happiness. If you knew what all those countries are that I have traversed, when compared with Italy!

The last thing that impressed me vividly and profoundly was Venice. You know how beautiful it is; therefore, I will not lay myself out in descriptions, nor in ecstasies — you understand me.

You have probably learned on your part, dear friend, of the death of our good comrade, Blanchard. It is by the sorrow this event caused me, that I judge what you must have felt — you, who were so much more intimately connected with him than I. So you see, my dear friend, how uncertain we are of seeing each other again when we separate, and, although nothing is more commonplace, there is nothing more terribly necessary to put at the bottom of each letter than:

Adieu, dear friend, adieu; I embrace you as I love you—that is to say, like a friend, like a brother, and always in the hope that we may meet again.

Adieu—yours with all my heart,
                    CHARLES GOUNOD.

IV.

MONSIEUR CHARLES GOUNOD,
        47 Rue Pigalle, Paris.

November 19th.

MY DEAR GOUNOD:

I have just read very attentively your choruses in *Ulysse*. The work, in its entirety, seems to me very remarkable, and the musical interest goes on increasing with that of the drama. The double chorus of the Banquet is admirable, and will produce an exciting effect if properly performed. The *Comédie-Française* neither ought, nor can be, niggardly with regard to your means of execution. According to my opinion, the music alone will attract the crowd for a great number of presentations. It is, then, in the most direct pecuniary interest of the director to allow to the musical composer a large part of the expense and of the stage-setting of *Ulysse;* and I think he will do so. But do not weaken in your demands. *It must be done in the right way*, or not at all. Be careful about the singers to whom you entrust your solos; a ridiculous solo spoils a whole piece.

On the page turned down at the corner is an error in punctuation in the music, at the commencement of a verse, that I advise you to correct. An artist should not scan in this way; leave that to cheap rhymesters.

A thousand warm and sincere compliments. Yours devotedly,

H. BERLIOZ.

V.

Monsieur Hector Lefuel,
20 Rue de Tournon, Paris.

My Dear Hector:
I went to your house, nearly a month ago, to inform you of a very important event, to the knowledge of which your ancient title of "friend and father" gives you a special right. I am going to be married next month, to Mademoiselle Anna Zimmerman. We are all perfectly satisfied with this union, which seems to offer the most reliable assurances of lasting happiness. The family is excellent, and I have the good luck to be loved by all its members.

I am sure, dear friend, that you will rejoice with me most heartily in this new happiness. It will be temporarily disturbed, however, by the cruel recalling to our poor Martha* of the same pleasure once tasted by her, the loss of which she now mourns daily. God grant that the affection of my new

---

* The widow of Gounod's brother.

companion may console her for the
unintentional pain roused in her heart
by the joy of this new sister! So it will
be, I trust; for these two good creatures
are already very sympathetic.

Adieu, **dear** Hector, with all my
heart.

CHARLES GOUNOD.

My affectionate regards to Madame
Lefuel.

VI.

MONSIEUR PIGNY,*
Rue d' Enghien, Paris.

LUCERNE, Tuesday,
August 28, 1855.

MY DEAR AND GOOD PIGNY:

In the letter received to-day from my
mother, she tells me with the thankful
feeling of an appreciative heart, of the
filial attentions you have shown her
since my departure, and of the delicate
precautions with which you offered to

---

* M. Pigny, architect, had also married a
daughter of Zimmerman.

surround her, by assisting personally in her removal from the country, a change always troublesome for one of her advanced years, however reduced the undertaking may be by the simplicity of her habits and of her life.

You who have, as they say, a mother Devotion, a mother Abnegation (I use these words purposely, as epithets do not suffice for hearts of this kind), you will understand me when I tell you that to give to my mother is to give to me what is sweetest and dearest; for it is to supplement and aid me in a work that I shall never accomplish as I wish; that is, to return to my mother a small part of what her long, honorable, and laborious life has lavished for me in cares, sacrifices, anxieties, and devotion of all kinds. In a word, we have been her whole life; she will have been but a part of ours.

Believe me, my dear Pigny, I am deeply touched at finding you already in relationship so sympathetic with me, and, in addition to the affection with which all regard you here, nothing could give you a better right and title to a place in my heart than the reverential deference you have so cordially shown to my honored and dearly beloved mother.

CHARLES GOUNOD.